T0150370

Women Who Misbehave

ADVANCE PRAISE FOR THE BOOK

'Sayantani Dasgupta's short stories are witty, well-crafted, and wondrous. Compulsively readable, Dasgupta's stories announce an exciting new talent in Indian fiction.'—Aruni Kashyap, writer and translator

'Sayantani Dasgupta's story collection, *Women Who Misbehave*, should win prizes. A very fine authority lives in the sentences; the language and structure are fresh. A reader sees, feels, smells and tastes the stories as if he/she is inside the scenes. Some of the characters and plots must have surprised the writer herself—they have that feel, that quality. On a larger scale, Dasgupta's stories can divine the uniqueness of a particular community, and as a body of work, they show us that (as a writer once said), "There is no country but the heart." Do not pass up this book'—Clyde Edgerton, author of *Raney* and *The Night Train*

'Sayantani Dasgupta's stories are bright, beautiful shards of glass. Each an experiment in form and narration, they work to carefully uncover our frailties, our contradictions, unveiling the small yet extraordinary lives of these women. Sayantani's voice is bold, courageous, at times wickedly funny, moving easily between the multitude of spaces her characters occupy, the domestic and familial, the neighbourly, the workplace, the romantic. These aren't all "nice" women—but they're real, and honest, and vulnerable, and you come away feeling for them as you would if you were to know them in real life'—Janice Pariat, author of *Seahorse*

'Sayantani Dasgupta is a mesmerizing storyteller, and *Women Who Misbehave* captivated me from the beginning. Whether writing about a contemporary woman contemplating the dark edges of her fate near the Texas–Mexico border or a pregnant young wife thinking of leaving her husband in the Calcutta of 1948, Dasgupta approaches her characters with compassion and fearless conviction. Wise and witty, infused with risk, mystery, loss and desire, as well as a whisper of horror and a dash of romance, these stories reveal a writer whose biting insight into human nature grows sharper with every page. Sayantani Dasgupta is a writer to watch'—Kim Barnes, author of *In the Kingdom of Men*

'Sayantani Dasgupta, in *Women Who Misbehave*, mercilessly annihilates the idea of the imaginary, illusive and perfect woman, and resurrects a species of unconventional women whom I [would] love to call real because they were born to upset and destroy the status quo. These women, some of them [appearing to be] deceptive porcelain dolls, "rely on the everyday minutiae of their own lives" to spin their worlds, [while] some others seem like bitter roshogollas who mar the taste of all that you have ever eaten, even as the rest appear to be like houses you have seen all your life, but who relentlessly guard their inner mystery. They leave you inspired and challenged, devastated and thrilled, all at the same time. Sayantani proves that shattering stereotypes is a dynamic and courageous political process'—K.R. Meera, writer and journalist

'Dasgupta's stories are emotional maps that allow the reader to find themselves curiously delighted in both familiar and unfamiliar territory. *Women Who Misbehave* celebrates the awkward and pretentious roads we take when we're unsure of the boxes we've been [made to] fit into. These women are unabashedly loud, confident, insecure, ambitious, careless and gloriously imperfect. This book is an invitation to jump time and geography while Dasgupta's adventurously contemporary prose ensures that we're compelled to find a part of ourselves in each one of these stories'—Rheea Mukherjee, author of *The Body Myth*

women who misbehave

short stories

SAYANTANI DASGUPTA

PENGUIN
VIKING
An imprint of Penguin Random House

VIKING

USA | Canada | UK | Ireland | Australia
New Zealand | India | South Africa | China

Viking is part of the Penguin Random House group of companies
whose addresses can be found at global.penguinrandomhouse.com

Published by Penguin Random House India Pvt. Ltd
7th Floor, Infinity Tower C, DLF Cyber City,
Gurgaon 122 002, Haryana, India

First published in Viking by Penguin Random House India 2021

Copyright © Sayantani Dasgupta 2021

10 9 8 7 6 5 4 3 2 1

ISBN 9780670094981

Typeset in Minion Pro by Manipal Technologies Limited, Manipal
Printed at Thomson Press India Ltd, New Delhi

www.penguin.co.in

For Amrinder,
who loves me, and lives with me,
despite knowing how I think

CONTENTS

AUTHOR'S NOTE

WHY I WROTE *WOMEN WHO MISBEHAVE*

As children, my brother and I would often recreate scenes from popular TV shows and movies for our entertainment. Because of our eight-year age difference, I towered over him; so naturally, I elected to play both the hero and the villain because they had the most to say in any situation. Whether it was avenging a father's murder, defending a sister's honour, saving peasants from evil landlords, reuniting with a long-lost sibling in this lifetime or the next, reincarnating to keep a promise made to a mother, helping the blind cross the road, saving the nation from terrorists, singing motivational songs to prisoners—whatever be the challenge, the men did it all, and with a dance routine or two thrown in for extra oomph.

My brother would be stuck playing the girlfriend, suffering sister, widowed mother, and so on. He protested, as anyone with any shred of dignity would, but because I was stronger and louder, my decision held.

Despite these challenges, I think it is safe to say that my brother has forgiven me. We remain close, and for that I am grateful. In 2015, on a trip home, he took me to watch the Ajay Devgn–Tabu starrer *Drishyam*. The trailer promised a battle of wits between two equally strong adversaries— Devgn, a clever but desperate father, and Tabu, a grieving mother and high-ranking police officer.

Did *Drishyam* turn out to be an engrossing film? Yes. Were the two adversaries equally strong? No. By the end of the movie, the audience gets to know Devgn's likes, dislikes, interests, his backstory and friends. His is a fully fleshed-out character with many facets. Tabu's, on the other hand, is one-dimensional. All you learn is that she's a power-hungry cop, a committed mother, and in a tense relationship with her husband. She is also given comparatively little screen time, no backstory, and we don't even get to know what contributed to her becoming a terrific police officer.

Though hers was a role far more interesting than most women I watched while growing up in the '80s and '90s, it still left much to be desired. It reminded me of the predictable category of the good girls, as opposed to the bad girls, and how societal standards and expectations, though thankfully not my own family's, had dictated that I emulate them. I should sacrifice for the sake of my husband or father or brother. I should cast my ambitions aside if my family's aspirations were at stake. I shouldn't drink or smoke because those habits would definitely make me a 'bad' girl.

I wrote *Women Who Misbehave* because when I was growing up, I needed more women to do the things the men were doing. I needed more than the handful of 'women-oriented' shows and movies, especially since they rarely went beyond exploring love, duty, family, home and sacrifice. I wanted women to give in to anger, ambition, wanderlust, desire, insecurity, greed, sloth and even perversity.

I hope the misbehaving women in this book do that for you. I hope they serve neither as heroes nor as villains, but look you straight in the eye from somewhere in the middle.

THE PARTY

It is a Friday evening, but you can't head home and settle in front of the TV with beers from your fridge and mutton biryani from the dhaba across the street. It's already been a long day and doesn't seem to be anywhere close to ending. You now have to go to your friend's home for a dinner party. Well, she isn't really a *friend*. She is a former colleague, so you *can* blow it off. But you're not an asshole, and she has invited you to celebrate the three-month anniversary of her wedding. You care neither for the occasion nor the husband. Still, you board an auto and head her way because you are a good person.

The two-storeyed bungalow-style home has a wrought-iron gate and a small garden. It is conveniently located a hop, skip and a jump from the bustling Hauz Khas market. You can't help being envious. They probably just stand on their balcony and holler for all sorts of vendors to come rushing with platters of pakoras, samosas and hot jalebis straight from the fryer. You, on the other hand, live in the hinterland by yourself because that's what you can afford on your salary. Which is really why you tip the dhaba boys so generously

3

every time they deliver your order. You cannot risk angering the one source of palatable food in your neighbourhood.

You reread the directions your friend texted you this morning. You are to go straight upstairs and neither loiter around the ground floor nor accidentally ring the bell. The husband's widowed mother lives on the ground floor, and you've been warned that she has little tolerance for anyone under the age of seventy.

You walk past the tidy square garden until you hit the mosaic staircase. With each step you take, the strain of jazz music grows stronger. The stairs lead you to a heavy black door, and you let your finger hover over the bell. You're no expert, you don't know the names and types of woods in this world, but you can tell *this* is expensive. And you're happy for your former colleague, you truly are. After all, how many people your age, and with practically the same goddamned salary, get to disappear behind a door like this every evening?

You take a deep breath and press the bell even though your throat feels like it is closing in, like flowers whose petals clam up at night. *We are done preening for you, sucker!*

You hear the momentary lull in conversation, but you have already recognized the voices. You quit these people a few months ago in pursuit of a flashier salary, but now you have to spend an entire evening with them. You press the doorbell again. Urgently. As if you are here to take care of serious business.

Tanu opens the door, her face awash with happiness. Marriage hasn't changed her, at least not on the outside. She is dressed simply in her usual blue jeans and a pale T-shirt, her outfit of choice for practically every occasion. She gives you a hug and you breathe in a cloud of familiar smells— lemon verbena soap, sandalwood perfume. Mahesh slides up beside her, his shaved head hovering like an egg over her bony shoulder, his arm possessively gripping her tiny waist. He smiles too and says, 'Welcome, welcome. Please come in.'

You say 'thank you' although you can't help but think that the deep lines under his eyes and the tight way his skin stretches over his face make him look less like Tanu's husband and more like a creepy uncle. Somehow, the fifteen-year gap between them is more pronounced this evening than it was on the day of their wedding, when you saw him for the first time. But you were too drunk then, and so all you remember is how after a few drinks Mahesh began telling everyone what he would like to do to every man who had ever hurt Tanu. You had giggled along with the others, but, secretly, you had wondered what it might feel like to be the object of such passion.

You catch Mahesh's eyes sweeping over your black shirt. His gaze doesn't linger on your breasts—maybe if you weren't so flat-chested things would be different—but out of habit, you surreptitiously glance down to check that the buttons haven't come undone.

'Black really suits you,' Mahesh says.

You laugh because you haven't mastered the art of accepting compliments. You follow Mahesh and Tanu into the drawing room where a cluster of familiar faces acknowledge you with varying degrees of nods and smiles.

It's a smartly put-together room—stainless steel and white leather, with tasteful accents of bamboo. Two love seats face an enormous couch and the side tables have neat stacks of expensive-looking coffee-table books, lit up just so by stark, Scandinavian-looking lamps.

On one of the love seats, Pia and Projapoti are smashed next to each other, gazing into a glossy book of black-and-white photographs of umbrellas. Their romance is as new as it is tumultuous, so you tell yourself to forgive them if they ignore you. But they don't. Pia looks up to give you a cheery wink and Projapoti, who took you under her wing when you first joined the company, sets downs her drink, stands up and wraps you in a hug.

Rani is sprawled on the couch. Swathed in a voluminous pink and red sari, she looks like a porcelain doll. Her eyes are closed; her lips are pressed together. She is the picture of calm, a far cry from the perpetually anxious person she is at work.

Auro, the only other man in the room besides Mahesh, is on the other end of the couch. He was hired to replace you, and you trained him during the last week that you were there. But from the cocky, two-fingered salute he gives you, you would think it was the other way round. He slides towards Rani to make space for you on the couch. You sit beside him, and as if to deliberately ignore your irritation, Auro stretches languorously and crosses his long legs at the ankles.

Tanu and Mahesh settle into the other love seat and resume their conversation with Auro, something about Nietzsche's third principle.

'I have never understood his point that if you stare at the abyss, the abyss stares back,' Auro says, taking a swig of his drink. 'I mean, I know what it means literally. You will become whatever you let consume you. But I think it is our ability to turn away from the abyss that makes us human.'

Mahesh leans back and sighs dramatically. You wonder if it's mostly for effect because he must sense the way Tanu looks at him, her eyes filled more with the ardour of a devotee than the love of a wife.

Rani, too, stares at Mahesh, as if in a daze. She moistens her parted lips and cups her chin, the way one does while admiring a work of art.

You, however, are too tired to care about what any of the men—Nietzsche, Mahesh or Auro—have thought or said. You glance around, hoping someone will offer you a drink or a bite to eat. But no one moves a muscle, as if this isn't your first time here, as if you didn't just arrive at a party hungry and tired after a long day at work.

You steal a look at your watch. It's only 6.30 p.m. You need something in your hands, if only to distract your rumbling stomach. You spot the stylish bar cart in the corner. There are two shelves lined with bottles of expensive liquor, a handful of glasses and two bowls of chips. You carefully avoid Auro's legs and walk over to pour yourself a generous drink. But where's the ice?

You're considering trying the kitchen when Mahesh calls out, 'Sorry. Our fridge broke this morning. So, no ice.'

It's April. In New Delhi. What kind of human beings invite people over with no fridge and no ice?

You return to the couch and sink in, grateful for the blast of the air conditioner in your face. Perhaps things aren't that dire after all. At least this is not the kind of party your new company likes to throw every Saturday, where you are required to spend the entire evening on your feet, balancing little bird-sized snacks in one hand and a drink in the other, all the while moving around the room, mingling with guests and holding forth on a variety of topics. Truth be told, you're bad at it, so you stick to the few faces you know, like an infant latched on to a warm teat.

Your stomach grumbles, loud enough for everyone to hear, but nobody does over the din of whatever Nietzsche did and didn't say. You wonder if there is a pleasant way to ask about food as you breathe in the oily, fried smells wafting in from the market outside. Surely, two bowls of potato chips cannot be it.

As if reading your mind, Tanu says, 'Mahesh suggested we keep the appetizers light. He is cooking dinner. Mutton biryani. It's his speciality.'

Wait. Is she calling potato chips appetizers? You consider asking her but then kill the question in your throat. You say something about how mutton biryani is your favourite food, and how nothing compares to the taste of tender meat layered with rice and spices and cooked over a low flame for hours. But how does Mahesh intend to cook something that indulgent and time-consuming this late? Even if he starts right this minute, when will he be done? When will everyone eat? But really, what do *you* know? You have never cooked mutton biryani. You have relied on restaurants, cheap and otherwise, to fulfil your need for the dish. Maybe Mahesh has mastered a shortcut.

You watch Pia close the big book of umbrellas and prop her head on Projapoti's shoulder. She plants mini kisses on Projapoti's neck. Your stomach churns. No, no, no, not again. You have watched enough lesbian PDA to last you a lifetime. When you first joined the company, it was Tanu and Projapoti who used to be an item. A few months later, they broke up but remained friends. Shortly after, Pia joined the team and she and Projapoti began dating. Or rather, slurping. Poor you! You had no choice in this matter. Your cubicle was right across from theirs. You had to watch them kiss open-mouthed and listen to their soft moans. It made you feel grateful that Tanu and Projapoti had been your first lesbians. They didn't kiss as frequently, nor did they make you that uncomfortable.

Which is why it was so easy—and nice—to imagine them together in bed, naked. It was a harmless pastime, really. It didn't mean anything. It certainly didn't mean *you* were a lesbian. If you were a man, you would have had no trouble liking Tanu's curly hair or brushing it away from her face. Or complimenting her beautiful smile and kissing the hollow at the base of her neck. But you aren't a man, and therefore, these thoughts are silly and pointless. Best to nip them in the bud.

The vodka has hit a sweet spot. It makes you want to try to focus on the conversation. Mahesh and Auro have moved away from Nietzsche and are now arguing over whether video games can be considered art. You don't know who believes what, and truth be told, you don't care. But once again, you notice the difference in the body language of the two men. Auro's face is pinched with effort. His nostrils are flared and he has leaned forward, waving his hands to fight for his point.

Mahesh, on the other hand, is still comfortably sitting. He has his right arm wrapped around his adoring wife. Every now and then, when he shifts, soft light bounces off his shaved head, giving him the appearance of an enlightened guru dispensing wisdom to his disciples.

A high-pitched, shrill giggle alerts you that Rani has finally opened her mouth in response to something Mahesh has said. She pushes her red-rimmed glasses to the top of her head and nods vigorously, pausing only to ask Tanu the location of the bathroom. When she gets up, you notice her walk, the deliberate swing in her hips, an invitation if ever there was one.

You aren't the only one who's been watching Rani watch Mahesh. Tanu has quietly refilled the bowls and is passing them around, but her eyes keep flitting back to Rani. You shovel a handful of chips into your mouth as you once again ignore the lustful cries of the vendors outside. You refill your glass even though you know you shouldn't drink any more on an empty stomach—but what else are you to do?

You remember the first time you witnessed a fight between Pia and Projapoti. It had started like a slow burn, over something as inconsequential as who should buy the next pack of beer, but it had quickly escalated into an inferno. Pia and Projapoti had flung accusations and counter-accusations. You wouldn't think they had been dating only a short while because the fight brought in every imaginable issue—money, house chores, feeding the cats, past fights, respective mothers. Projapoti had pounded her fists on her desk and smashed the computer mouse, while Pia had marched out to the pebbled driveway, where, armed with her dark glasses and a pack of cigarettes, she had paced in a frenzy.

In spite of that scene, two weeks later, Pia and Projapoti had opted to move in together. It was a one-bedroom apartment with a sliver of a balcony facing a golf course.

You had heard about it the Monday after they threw their house-warming party. They had invited everyone, including you, but you had pleaded a headache and rushed home instead. Why put yourself through additional discomfort anyway? It was enough to hear Projapoti's Harley Davidson pull into the office driveway every morning with Pia perched on the back, her tight ass pointed to the sky like a dare.

Mahesh finally says the words you have been waiting to hear since you got here. 'Let's get down to dinner, shall we?' he says, smacking his right knee theatrically with a sharp thwack.

You steal another glance at your watch. It's a little past eight. Had you been home, you would have demolished the dhaba biryani by now along with a Netflix movie. Still, you are too well brought up to not offer help. 'Do you need a sous-chef?' you ask before you can stop yourself.

As always, you are the only fool who has offered to help. That too in a hot kitchen in April in New Delhi. And on an empty stomach. The other guests are absorbed in each other or their phones. Maybe Mahesh will thank you profusely and ask you to sit down.

No such luck. Mahesh's egg-shaped head gleams like a pearl. He grins, 'Yes, of course. Could you slice some onions for me? And then the garlic?' He stops Tanu from following him into the kitchen. 'Not you, my sweets. Not tonight. Tonight, you get full release from the kitchen.'

Tanu gives Mahesh a quick peck on the cheek. She asks 'Are you sure?' so sweetly that it crushes your heart. When she returns to her spot in the drawing room, you watch her clasp her hands, as if she doesn't know what to do with this wealth of affection.

Mahesh hands you three enormous onions and clears a space for you on the black stone kitchen countertop. A childhood memory slides into your mind. You were nine years old, and it was the day of the annual Christmas party at school. Like the previous years, you and your friends had brought food from home to share with each other. You had sat in a large circle and passed around platters of bread rolls and samosas, bags of chips and biscuits, and tiffin boxes filled with laddus and barfis. Someone had brought a tray of cucumber sandwiches. By the time the tray had made its way over to you, there were only three sandwiches left. The two girls sitting with you had grabbed theirs quickly, leaving you with the last one on the tray. That poor sandwich hadn't kept its shape. It had collapsed in the middle. You had hesitated; the dismembered sandwich hadn't looked appetizing, but overcome by greed and curiosity, you had scooped it up. The girl next to you had nodded sagely and said, 'You did the right thing. You loved the ugly stepchild.' For some reason, hearing those words had made your heart swell with pride.

Later, at home, you had narrated the story to your parents over dinner. Granted, it was a small story but still, you had thought they would be proud that you didn't get caught up with the appearance of something as insignificant as a sandwich. You no longer remember what your mother served for dinner that night or what else the three of you talked about. But long after everyone had gone to bed, when you had got up to go to the kitchen for water, you had overheard your mother hissing to your father, 'I cannot believe I gave birth to a spineless child.'

Although slicing the onions does not take more than fifteen minutes, you emerge from the kitchen two hours later. Your feet are so tired that you can barely stand. Every time you made a move to withdraw from the kitchen and return to the drawing room, Mahesh began yet another topic of discussion. Except it was never a discussion. It was him listening to his own voice spread wisdom on topics as wide-ranging as the best writing software on the market, why the rhino population might be on the rise in Kaziranga, who was the better president between Kennedy and Nixon, and what really differentiated Marxist philosophy from Leninist.

You notice the guests have rearranged themselves. Projapoti and Tanu are now on the big, white leather couch, and Rani, Pia and Auro are stretched out on the floor. You collapse on the nearest love seat. If you stretch your legs, your toes will brush against Auro's thigh. The alcohol makes you want to try it although he is staring intently at his phone. At the very least, you want to say something smart so he will take notice.

But you can't because you have never been charming, and right this minute, the inside of your mouth tastes like chalk. You are most definitely the only one in this room still a virgin. Sure, you have gone on a few dates and those men have slipped their hands under your shirts. But that's as far as you've allowed it, paralysed by your childhood fear of getting pregnant the first time you sleep with someone, the way it always happens in Hindi films.

The sight of Projapoti and Tanu on the couch reminds you of when they used to be a couple. Although that was many months ago—and back then you knew far less about lesbians than you know now—their relationship made sense. They agreed easily, like a husband and wife married for decades. They were so attuned to each other's needs; they were intuitive to a fault and boring in their predictability. Their relationship lacked the ravenous passion that Projapoti's relationship with Pia oozed from the start.

Wait, did Auro say something? Did he say something to *you*?

'What?' you blurt through the alcohol-induced stupor in your head. In spite of the other conversations unfolding around you, your question comes out louder than what is socially acceptable.

'What are you doing afterwards?' Auro asks, a touch of impatience in his voice, in a tone so low that you can hardly hear.

You shrug, fearful and desperate at the same time, itching to grasp the opportunity but also horrified at where it might lead you.

You don't realize that Mahesh has come out of the kitchen and slid in to the spot beside you. 'Surely, you aren't thinking of leaving?' he asks you loudly. 'You came in after everyone else.' He wags his finger in your face, 'You *have* to stay.'

'Of course,' the words tumble out of you automatically, even as an angry, bitter taste fills your mouth. Auro looks away. *No, Ma, I was not spineless.*

Finally, it's time to eat. You are not used to eating this late. You have lost your appetite. Still, not wanting to seem rude or inconsiderate, you load up a plate. The browned rice and meat smell excellent, but the first bite proves disappointing. As does the second and the third. And so on. If this is Mahesh's speciality, you don't want to be in the kitchen when he is in a bad mood. The undercooked rice does no favours to the meat, which is horribly fibrous in places. Everything is so over-salted that you probably won't have to consume any sodium for the next five years. The onions, burnt and greasy, stick to the roof of your mouth, and the hard grains of rice feel like pebbles on your teeth.

Pia and Projapoti share a plate. They feed each other little bites, praising the biryani like it is the best thing they have put into their mouths. They waste most of what they ladle out on their plate and leave without waiting for anyone else to finish.

Auro, too, takes off soon after. He shakes Mahesh's hand, thanks him profusely, then kisses Tanu's cheek.

When he says goodbye to you, his smile is brief. His eyes are neither cold nor cruel, but they are filled with pity, the kind one might reserve for a wretched dog. He offers Rani a lift and she takes it.

Now, there are only three people left—Tanu, Mahesh and you. Mahesh refills his glass and yours.

When you look at Tanu inquiringly, she smiles. 'We're trying to get pregnant. My ob-gyn has prescribed hormone pills. I'm off booze these days.'

'So, what have you been drinking the whole evening?'

'Mostly water. Some orange juice. I'm also prone to dehydration, so I have to build better habits.'

'Don't you miss it?'

'Miss it? Oh my god, I can't tell you what I'd do for an ice-cold beer in this heat.'

'I can't wait to be a dad,' Mahesh says, beaming. 'Ever since the pills, we've doubled our efforts. I'm drinking less to boost my bad boys.'

You wince. *TMI*, you want to shout.

Mahesh laughs. He has no use for your prudishness. He pulls Tanu close and plants a wet kiss on her mouth. You see his lips at work as he buries his long fingers in her hair.

When they finally pull apart, Tanu cups his face with her hands. 'I don't think you recognize your own attractiveness, Mahesh. Did you see how Rani was looking at you? She wants you. Don't you see it?' Tanu's voice trembles and she looks at you for corroboration.

Mahesh's eyes soften. In that moment, he is no longer a man with an egg-shaped head, obsessed with the sound of his own voice. He is also not the uncouth revenge freak you met on the day of their wedding, eager to wreak devastation on the boys and men who'd hurt Tanu in the past, and whose names and last names he claimed to have memorized to ensure that if life ever brought them to him, he would be sure to tear them apart.

The clench in your throat makes you realize that you are looking at a vulnerable man, a man frightened that he might lose what he loves most in his life. But then the vodka acts up. At least that's how you justify your words for days afterwards, when you realize again and again what you have done. You blame it on a number of things— the broken fridge, the iceless pours of vodka that you drank on an empty stomach, the terrible biryani, the ego behind Mahesh's conversations, the way Auro suggested something and since you were too chicken to take it, how he offered it to Rani, and she took it.

You are done being that nine-year-old kid who got the dismembered sandwich. You are done disappointing your mother with your spinelessness. You cannot stand another moment of being a virgin, or the thought of being the useless fuck you would have been for Auro, although a part of you wishes you had gone ahead with it, just this once.

And so you ignore the warning inside your head, the eerie stillness of caution that matches the empty streets below, where the vendors have long since packed up for the night, and you smile sweetly and say, 'Tanu, does it feel weird watching Projapoti with another woman?'

You watch Tanu's face as it loses colour, as her cheekbones turn gaunt and hollow like a bird's. She has never discussed this matter with you, but you have always guessed this about Mahesh. He has never known about Tanu's relationship with Projapoti. In spite of all his talk and intellectual bullshit, Mahesh is the kind of man who cannot stomach the idea of his wife ever having been satisfied by a woman.

You are not the only one to come to this realization. Tanu holds your gaze until you cannot bear it any more and have to look away. She carefully sets down her orange juice. She refuses to look at Mahesh even though he is right there, his body straight, his face unmoving and his head full of the names of men he wants to beat up to protect his wife.

Tanu gets up from the sofa and sinks into the love seat where Pia and Projapoti sat not too long ago. From the side table, she picks up Pia's half-empty glass of vodka and takes a sip.

A HARD
KIND OF
LOVE

Misha and Neel met at the launch of the anthology *Twenty Under Thirty*, a collection of stories by twenty of India's most promising writers under the age of thirty. Neel was standing in line for food, absent-mindedly picking at his beard. He consulted his watch for the fourth time in ten minutes. Food, a little meet-and-greet, then home—that was his plan. These after-work, mandatory events were the worst. He didn't care whose protagonist was 'edgy' or whose writing was 'for the generations'. The last book he had read was probably *Who Moved My Cheese*? Sure, he worked in a publishing house, but he was an accountant. And a damn good one at that. He wished he could skip book launches, but he knew that wouldn't sit well with his boss.

When he saw her approach the line, Neel straightened. He stopped fiddling with his beard. Not that she was conventionally attractive. *But still.* She was dressed in an orange blouse and black jeans, a striking combination on her small frame. He recognized her from the photographs of the contributors on the back cover of *Twenty Under Thirty*.

Not many days ago, when his colleagues had left and he was stuck in front of his computer fixing an Excel sheet, he had glanced at the faces of all the female writers. He vaguely remembered finding her attractive.

As if to check out the art on the wall behind her, Neel half-turned to get a better look. She had full lips but a hard chin, small tits but a nice-enough ass. Her short hair framed her face. *Definitely attractive.* He ran a hand over his thinning hair, as if that might restore his long-lost, crowning glory. At least he could improve his posture. He squared his shoulders and stood straight.

'Hello,' she smiled brightly, 'are you one of the contributors?'

'No. I am a mere accountant.'

'At Ink & Blot?'

'At Ink & Blot.'

She gave the briefest of nods and scanned the crowd, searching for familiar faces. Had he already bored her? When he reached the spread, Neel loaded his plate with crackers, fried cubes of paneer and mini kebabs. He sensed she didn't know anyone. It would be rude to walk away, wouldn't it? He hovered uncertainly, wary of coming across as a creep.

She filled up her plate and gestured towards one of the empty tables in a corner. 'Join me?' she asked. And added, 'I'm Misha.'

They refilled their small plates twice. When she stepped out to take a call, he brought over two beers and a bottle of water. He told her about his childhood, his ancestral home in Shillong and how he missed its rains the most. At one point, he winced. 'I am boring you, am I not? I must be boring you. I haven't let you say more than five words.'

Misha raised a hand in protest. 'No, no. Please carry on. I love listening to people's stories, and yours are fascinating.'

'Really?'

'Yes. *I* am the one who's boring. I have never lived anywhere but Delhi. Hell, I have never even lived by myself.'

'What do your parents do?'

'They are both professors at JNU.'

'Wow.'

'Yeah. Everyone in my family loves to read and write. I am not that original or trailblazing in their eyes,' Misha laughed.

Neel shook his head. 'I am sure that's not true. You seem plenty original to me.'

Misha blushed and looked away.

He hoped that she saw he wasn't trying to flatter her. She was different from the 'creative types' he often came across. For one, she wasn't full of herself. Second, she was easy to talk to. Third, she was interested in him, in his stories. She told him about her day job—as the arts and culture commentator for a newspaper—and about the book she was writing.

'My first novel. I have only written the first chapter,' she tapped her chin. 'Don't get me wrong. I love my job and it's great to be included in this "Twenty Under Thirty" list, but I wish I could stay home for three months straight and finish my book.'

'What's it about?' Neel asked, regretting it immediately. If he had learned anything from book launches, it was that writers got asked this question the most. He had never paid attention to their answers before, but Misha's he wanted to know. 'You don't have to answer if you don't want to,' he said. 'It is the most predictable question, isn't it?' He was surprised by how badly he wanted her approval.

'That's all right. I struggle to explain what my novel is about. I need the practice.' Misha took a deep breath. 'So, it's weird and dystopian. Each of the main characters needs to have three major crises—social, environmental and personal.'

'How many crises do they have so far?'

'None. One if lucky.'

They both laughed at that.

The evening ended with them exchanging numbers. When he pulled out his flip phone, Misha's eyes widened with surprise. 'You must be the only person in this room with this antique piece,' she said.

'Easily!'

'What's the story here? Why don't you have a smartphone?'

'I find smartphones terrifying. Too much power in one click.'

'I think there's a story here you aren't telling . . .'

Neel's throat tightened. Was he this easy to read?

'No problem,' Misha continued, raising her hands as if to placate him. 'I have no problem with people holding on to their secrets. I think it's only fair. Because when you share your secret with someone, it's no longer a secret, and it's not yours any more. The listener can do with it what she pleases.'

'You are a dangerous person,' Neel said, his eyebrows raised.

'Well,' Misha shrugged, 'I *am* a writer.'

They met the following week for lunch, and after that for dinner. Before they knew it, they had become a 'thing'. One night, after they ate at a Chinese restaurant, Neel returned home and examined his apartment. He had purchased it fairly recently—two bedrooms, one and a half bathrooms, a tiny balcony overlooking a park.

Overall, he liked the space. It was walking distance to the nearest market, and only five kilometres from his office. For the first time though, he noticed the ordinariness of the bamboo chairs in the drawing room, the absence of nice curtains, the lumpy mattress he had had since graduating from college seven years ago and the chipped dining table where he ate his meals and replied to emails.

He made himself a cup of tea and walked out to the balcony. A couple was walking its yippy Pomeranian in the park in spite of signs that said 'No Pets Allowed'. Rule breakers made Neel angry, especially if they also owned tiny dogs. What was the point? If you wanted something small and furry, why not get a squirrel? He wondered what Misha thought of dogs. He wondered what she thought of children, and if she wanted any of her own.

Six months later, Neel and Misha got married and she moved into his apartment. She began accompanying Neel to each of Ink & Blot's book launches and author events. For Neel, these evenings took on a new meaning. Earlier, he had negotiated the world of books and publishing like a blind man, fumbling through conversations, but now, thanks to his brand-new wife, he knew whose book was coming out next, who received what signing amount, who was sleeping with whose editor, who could not hold on to a permanent job or write without getting drunk. His ears lapped up words he had paid only scant attention to in the past, words such as 'point of view', 'narrative arc' and 'protagonist'.

There were changes inside his apartment too. Misha converted the spare bedroom into her study. He watched her remove the Lakshmi–Ganesh calendar from the wall and replace it with large, black-and-white photographs of writers she admired. He recognized Ismat Chughtai and Toni Morrison, but the other three remained unknown.

Misha bought a new desk, and Neel watched as the movers hauled away the old one. Constructed of poor-quality wood and metal, it had been a cheap, second-hand purchase. But it had served him well. He had lost count of how many nights he had fallen asleep with his head on it. When he had woken up, his neck had felt tight and cramped like a tennis ball.

He had also lost his virginity against that desk. He could see that moment so clearly. It was Malati, his junior from college, the one with the eyes that always sparkled and smiled. He remembered her fleshy arms, the slightly dank smell of her armpits, the coffee breath she had heaved on to his face. And yet, he had been so eager. So grateful. He thought of the way Malati's eyes had lit up, how she had giggled afterwards and how, post dinner, he had helped her find a taxi home.

Neel swiftly moved his thoughts along. He didn't want to dwell on Malati. That was ancient history. With Misha, he wasn't going to mess things up. He purposefully followed her into the study and watched as she placed inkpot-shaped bookends on her new desk.

'I have so many beautiful notebooks,' Misha said. 'Gifts from friends, you know? Finally, they will be together.' She grouped them into neat stacks and slid them into drawers. All through the afternoon, she arranged her desktop computer, the printer and several items of stationery. She lined up her dictionary, thesaurus and other heavy books between the bookends.

Neel thought they looked like obedient students. He smiled. This brilliant, smart, hard-working creature was his wife. Why then was he being sentimental over an old desk?

A few weeks later, Misha quit her job. When she announced it to her college friends over brunch, the women's reactions were swift and expected.

'What the hell happened?'

'They loved you in that office, didn't they?'

'Why didn't you at least talk to someone first?'

'How does Neel feel about this?'

If Misha felt hesitant to answer, she didn't show it. She broke a piece of garlic bread and shoved it into her mouth. 'Neel is fine with it,' she said, shrugging. 'He is the one who urged me to take this step.'

'Why?'

'Because I will finally have time to finish my novel.'

The women glanced at each other and dropped the subject. Later, each one of them called the others. They insisted that they could already see Misha's future, a life of predictable domesticity punctuated by two kids in quick succession. 'Another one bites the dust,' they sighed. In their texts to Misha, however, they wrote, 'Best of luck, sweetie. Can't wait for your book!'

Misha read the texts and rested her head on Neel's chest. 'Sometimes I hate my friends. I know what they are thinking. They are so sure that I will sink without a trace.'

Neel kissed her forehead. 'Truth be told, I do wish you had talked to me before quitting.'

Misha jerked her head up. 'What?' Her eyes narrowed. 'Come on,' she said. 'I thought you would be happy for me. I have been counting on your support, Neel. You *know* my book is *the* most important thing to me. If I had known you were going to behave like everyone else's husband, I would have continued slaving at my desk job.'

'Sorry, sorry, babe,' Neel pleaded. 'I didn't think this through.'

'Art takes time. Commitment. It's not something you can do while straddling a million things.'

Neel agreed. 'I know. I am so sorry. You did the right thing. I was being stupid.' He kissed his wife and stroked her back until she drifted off to sleep.

One evening, after they returned home from yet another Ink & Blot event—the launch of Survi Duggal's novel *Under a Purple Sky*—Neel rubbed his temples and complained. 'I have the worst headache. I hope I can sleep it off.' He wished they hadn't stayed out for so long. He brushed his teeth, washed his face and climbed under the sheets. Someone, either a toddler or a blacksmith, had barged into his head and was pounding the insides of his skull. 'Misha,' he said, 'will you get me a painkiller, please?'

Misha was at the dressing table. She had already removed her jewellery and was now wiping off her make-up. 'What did you think of Survi's reading?' she asked.

Neel rubbed his forehead. He had zoned out the second Survi had described her main character as 'parsimonious'. 'Good?' he offered.

'No! Don't say that. It was so over the top.'

'I thought you liked Survi? You called her first chapter "fearless".'

'I talked about the first chapter because that's all I read.'

'But I thought you liked Survi,' Neel repeated stupidly.

'Oh god, no. Her writing is terrible; she is terrible. I can bet you good money that Survi knows she is a hack. This book is destined to fail. Mark my words.'

'But don't you tell people that writing a book and having it published are massive accomplishments? That sales and awards don't matter. I have heard you say this multiple times.'

'Yes. But this *is* a bad book. It's not going to change the world.'

'And yours will?' The question escaped Neel's mouth before he could stop himself.

Misha didn't say anything. But a shadow crept into her eyes and clouded her face. Neel stiffened. He could see he had unnerved something deep inside Misha, something small but important, like the last piece of a jigsaw puzzle. He reached out. 'I am only teasing you, sweetheart. Your book will rival Rushdie's. The Roys, Naipauls and Chaudhuris will not know what hit them.'

Misha gave him a wan smile. 'Thanks,' she said, but her voice had lost its spunk.

'Come here, let me make things better,' Neel said. He pulled Misha towards him, and with deft fingers, kneaded her back and shoulders. He stroked her hair until he heard a light, fluttery snore. Only then did he climb out of bed and get himself a painkiller.

It was Friday the next day. Neel was alone at home. The doorbell rang in the afternoon. He answered it to find a tall woman, about Misha's age, waiting at the door. She had short, no-nonsense hair, and no make-up except for a bright swath of red lipstick. She had a navy-blue silk scarf tied loosely around her neck.

'Yes?' Neel asked.

'Is Misha here? I am Ruhi. We were in college together. You must be Neel.'

'Oh, hello! Please come in. I am sorry I didn't recognize you. Misha is out, but she should be back soon.'

'No need to apologize! You and I have never met. I am sorry I couldn't make it to the wedding. I wasn't in town. I am here for two days, so I thought I'd stop by and surprise Misha.'

Neel heated up pakoras in the microwave and served them with ketchup, mint chutney and steaming cups of black tea. Ruhi told him about how she became a pilot, how often she and Misha used to bunk classes in college, and how Dr Rao had once caught them smoking in the library.

Neel laughed. 'You are a superb storyteller. Do you write too?'

Ruhi pouted, drawing attention to her red lips. 'I wish! Not everyone's as talented as your wife, Neel. My problem is, I can't sit still long enough. When will I string ten sentences together?'

When Misha returned, Neel left the two friends alone. He withdrew to the kitchen to make more tea. Over the whirring of the exhaust fan, he heard their laughter. He arranged the cups and saucers on the tray, and when he had almost reached the drawing room, he overheard Misha. 'Good grief, Ruhi! That's like a man in every port! Aren't you the lucky one?'

He entered right when Ruhi was about to say something. Her cheeks flushed, almost matching the shade of her lips. Neel handed them the tea and left the room. What did he care if Ruhi had lovers in every city? He didn't know her. Sure, she had beautiful lips and an athletic body. So what? He had a gorgeous wife.

That night, however, Neel dreamed of Ruhi. He imagined the two of them inside a cockpit. Ruhi was dressed in a crisply ironed uniform and peaked cap. They were facing each other when the plane lurched and Ruhi toppled backwards, her arms splayed apart, eyes wide with fear. He rushed to help. He cried out her name in his sleep. 'Ruhi, careful!'

Neel woke up to Misha's hand shaking him. The light by her bedside table was on, a book was spreadeagled on her lap.

'What's going on?' Misha asked. 'Did you have a bad dream? Why were you crying out Ruhi's name?'

Neel reached for the glass of water on his nightstand. Haltingly, he told Misha about his dream. Nothing remotely sexual or romantic had happened, and yet he couldn't bring himself to meet her gaze. He tried. He knew that avoiding her eyes made him look guilty. 'Believe me,' he said again and again, 'the dream meant nothing.'

Misha laughed. 'Don't worry, darling. Ruhi has always been a bit of a slut. Go back to sleep.' She swung her legs off the bed and turned off her reading light.

'Where are you going?'

'I want to write. Go to sleep. We will talk in the morning.'

Neel closed his eyes and burrowed his head into the pillow, grateful for Misha's ability to see his silly dream for what it was.

In the bright light of the morning, Neel's dream embarrassed him even more. Misha poured him his cup of coffee and filled his bowl with cornflakes. He hoped had forgotten about the incident.

She sat across from him and slowly sipped her coffee. 'Tell me, Neel,' she began. 'If you aren't attracted to Ruhi, why do you think you dreamed about her? What does she mean to your subconscious?'

'She means nothing,' Neel looked up with a start. 'Please don't subject me to any weird analysis. I am not one of your fictional characters.'

'Okay,' Misha said, smiling. 'Do you want some more cornflakes?'

Neel shook his head and shovelled the last spoonful into his mouth. He felt Misha studying him, as if he was a specimen. It occurred to him that her question wasn't a result of jealousy. To her, in that moment, Neel was not her husband but a character who had veered off the track that had been set for him.

He packed a sandwich for lunch and left. When he returned nine hours later, he could hear the sharp rat-tat-tat of Misha's keyboard on full speed inside the study. He tried peeping, but the door was locked. He washed and changed, and then he brewed a fresh pot of tea. He returned to the study and knocked.

'Yes?' Misha's voice floated towards him as if from another planet.

'I made tea, sweetheart. Would you like some?'

'No. Thank you. Go away, please. I am writing.'

Neel hesitated for a second and then withdrew to the balcony. When Misha still hadn't stepped out by dinnertime, he heated up the leftovers and watched reruns of *Breaking Bad* until he dozed off on the sofa. Sometime after midnight, he woke up to Misha passionately kissing his face.

'What time is it?' he asked groggily. 'What are you doing? Are you done writing?'

'Shh . . . doesn't matter,' Misha whispered. She nibbled his ear and grazed her teeth against his neck. 'Come,' she said. 'Tell me you want this.' Her voice was suffused with longing. She had never sounded like this before. She undressed quickly and pressed his hands to her breasts.

'Are you sure?' Neel asked, now fully awake. 'Do you want to go to the bedroom at least?' Her lips tasted of peanut butter and he could smell the slight grease in her hair. Clearly, she hadn't showered in a couple of days.

'No, here is fine,' Misha said urgently.

~

For the next two weeks, Misha wrote like a maniac. She barely slept for four hours each day. She wrote nearly every minute that she was awake. She sacked the help (*too noisy and erratic, I can do it myself*). But then dishes began piling up in the sink, awaiting Neel's return every evening.

Soon, he had to take over breakfasts as well. When he packed his lunch, he packed for Misha too. He knew that if he didn't, she would only eat peanut butter. They began ordering in every night, alternating between Chinese, Mughlai and pizza.

When it finally seemed like he was living with a robot, Misha emerged from the study, her eyes tired but gleaming. She held up her arms triumphantly. 'It's done. I have sent it off.'

'The new story? Congratulations!' Neel said happily. 'What's it about?'

'I am not telling. Read it once it's published.'

'So, what can we do to celebrate?' Neel asked, kissing her neck.

'Nothing. Not right now,' Misha said, pushing him away. 'I need to shower and cook us a decent meal. This place is filthy!'

~

The esteemed European magazine *The Fog* published Misha's short story 'The Parrot Wife'. When the envelope arrived with a generous cheque and two complimentary copies, only Neel was at home. He poured himself some Scotch and settled down on the sofa to read. In the introduction, the editor had singled out Misha's story for praise. He had called her the new Margaret Atwood. Neel nodded appreciatively. He had never read anything by Margaret Atwood, but he knew his wife was brilliant. He dove in.

When he emerged on the other side of the story, Neel closed the magazine and left it on the coffee table. He tugged at his shirt collar. In spite of the breeze coming in from the balcony, his brow was clammy and his cheeks felt warm. He hadn't realized that everything that happened to Misha, including everything involving him and their marriage, was fair game for a story. Nothing was sacred or private or exclusively his any more. He closed his eyes and went over

'The Parrot Wife' in his head. He wanted to make sure he wasn't overreacting or imagining things.

Rik and Pia are young, in love and newly married. One night, as he is making love to his wife, Rik calls her by his ex-girlfriend's name. When he realizes his mistake, he tries to make amends by calling out Pia's name over and over again. Pia moans with pleasure. It seems as if she hasn't noticed her husband's faux pas, and a relieved Rik shrugs off his embarrassment. He swears to never make such a colossal mistake again.

On the six-month anniversary of their wedding, Pia surprises Rik by booking a luxury suite in the most expensive hotel in town. After they check in, Pia excuses herself to go to the bathroom. Rik turns on the TV. He is about to order a round of drinks and appetizers when Pia emerges from the bathroom. She has changed out of her jeans and T-shirt into a crimson negligee. Rik turns off the TV.

Pia pulls out the various tools and contraptions she has packed for their weekend. She lays them, one by one, on the bedside table. Her movements are brisk but careful, like a surgeon's. Rik eyes the handcuffs, the scented oils and lubes and the box of expensive chocolates.

'Strip,' Pia snaps her fingers and orders.

'But I want to do this slowly. I want to take care of you.'

'No,' Pia shakes her head. 'Strip.'

Rik doesn't need to be told twice. He moves like a man possessed and undresses swiftly.

Pia pushes him against the headboard and slowly rubs her naked body against his. In one smooth move, she handcuffs Rik to the bedpost. He licks his lips. He likes where things are going. Pia dives into her bag again. This time she pulls out a set of speakers. His toes tingle. 'Ah, music. I guess we haven't tried that yet.' He is eager for whatever Pia has chosen for them.

Pia unplugs the hotel phone and places it on the floor. She turns on the speakers. At first, there is only silence. Then, static. Finally, Rik hears a word. The volume is so low that he cannot hear it clearly. The word repeats itself, again and again, on loop. He looks up, confused. 'What's this?' he asks. 'A parrot? Where's the music?'

Pia turns up the volume. It's her voice. She is saying the name of Rik's former lover, his ex-girlfriend. 'What the fuck?' Rik protests. He pulls against the handcuffs, but his wrists are securely in place. Smiling, Pia watches him, the way one might watch a circus performance. She dives into her bag again and pulls out a wide strip of tape. Rik kicks hard, but Pia effortlessly seals his mouth. He strains against the handcuffs again, his wrists turning red from the effort. She clamps a pair of headphones, attached to the speakers, to his ears. His eyes bulge as she turns up the volume. The name of his ex-girlfriend *thrums through his body like it is the only sound in the universe. Slowly, Pia slips out of her negligee and puts on her jeans and T-shirt. She blows Rik a kiss. She grabs her purse, says 'I'll be back when you have learned your lesson' and shuts the door behind her.*

That night, Neel and Misha had their first big fight. Neel didn't sleep at all. He couldn't believe that his one slip-up had made its way into a story. 'Why did the whole world need to know?' he asked. 'I feel naked, Misha. Everyone will know it's me.'

For her part, Misha waved her hand, mouthed a sorry that didn't quite sound genuine and went off to sleep.

For the next two years, Misha's writing successes were as regular as the seasons. They spanned the entire breadth of the seven deadly sins—lust, gluttony, greed, sloth, wrath, envy, pride. Her work got anthologized several times, she got featured in renowned journals and was invited to speak at literary festivals.

If he felt violated by the number of times their marital experiences ended up in magazines for other people's enjoyment, Neel didn't say so. He had made peace with this aspect of his life. Surely, this is how all writers function. They rely on the everyday minutiae of their own lives to spin their stories.

Besides, this situation had its advantages. Every time Misha completed a story, they had a week of great sex, and what's more, she transformed into a domestic goddess. She cleaned every inch of the house; she sifted through recipes and cooked up a storm; they went out and socialized with friends. She sent gifts to his parents in Shillong and called them for hour-long phone conversations. She invited her own parents over for dinner. At night, she snuggled close to Neel and talked longingly about their future children. Until the idea of the next story sailed into her mind.

Then once again, it was a firmly closed door, scoops of peanut butter, hastily made sandwiches, a neglected house and an unwashed wife. In moments like these, when he felt sorry for himself, Neel reigned himself in by remembering Malati. She, the one with the flabby arms. She, who loved him. He remembered their last day together, the words he said, the hurt he cast into her eyes. It made him swallow the words he wanted to say to Misha.

In the fourth year of their marriage, Misha finally took on the labour of her life—her novel. It was dystopian, interspersed with quotes by Rumi and Descartes. Misha called it 'part mythology, part science fiction'. For months, she lived the life of a hermit. She wrote non-stop. She turned down friends' invitations. When Neel complained or begged her to accompany him to his office parties, she did so, but grudgingly. Eventually, she stopped doing even that. She cancelled on friends' book launches. When Neel tried to talk to her, she cried. 'They are all writing the same books whereas I am trying to do something new here.

You have to give me time.' When he raised the subject of children, she said, 'Soon.' He knew it meant, 'Once the novel is done.'

They celebrated when she finished. Clocking at nearly 400 pages, she had written and rewritten each paragraph close to thirty times. When she brought the manuscript out of the study to show Neel, he was in the kitchen, making coffee. When she pressed the manuscript into his hands, he kissed her cheek. He didn't know what to say. He had never pursued anything in his life with such deliberation. To celebrate her achievement, he cooked lamb with mint jelly, wild rice and a garden salad on the side.

Misha sent her novel to six publishing houses. After he returned from work in the evenings, Neel worked on Misha's website. She had hired a stylist and a photographer and got herself new headshots in anticipation of the author photos she believed she would soon be asked to provide.

Two months later, the first rejection email arrived. Others followed in quick succession. They all said similar things. 'Too dark', or 'too experimental'. One editor cut into her. 'Where's the talent you show in your short stories? Write something we can sell.'

Misha rewrote the whole thing and submitted it again. This time she had made the novel more realistic and less experimental. She had chiselled each word to a shine. She sent it to nine publishers. One wrote back suggesting changes. Three never replied. Five said, 'No, thank you.'

She tossed the novel into the bottom drawer of her desk, letting the rest of it fill up with old receipts and bills. When Neel suggested a holiday, somewhere, anywhere, out of Delhi, perhaps a week in the mountains of Shillong, Misha shook her head. She assured him she was fine. In the mornings, when he left for work, she would still be sleeping, hands tightened into fists, drool crusting her chin.

One night, long after they had gone to bed, Neel woke up to the neighbour's car alarm. When he turned to check on Misha, a jolt of electricity ran through him. It made the hair on the back of his neck stand. Misha's eyes were upon him, but it was not the loving gaze of a spouse. Neither was it the irritable face of someone jarred awake. Her eyes were blank as if she didn't know who she was or where she was and what she was doing. She looked like Malati had on her last day with him. Neel shook Misha's shoulder. Once, twice, thrice, until she blinked and came out of it, whatever that 'it' was.

All night long, Neel stayed awake. A throbbing pain built up and pulsed from his temples. He remembered Malati. He wondered what she thought of him now, if she ever thought of him at all, or of the time they had spent together.

It was an honest mistake that had laid the foundation of the end of his journey with Malati. Smartphones had just entered the market. They were new, easy, exciting. By then, he and Malati had been together for two years, and every few weeks he brought up the topic of marriage. That was the natural progression of things, wasn't it? Plus, they were compatible, they had fun, they liked each other's friends. What more could one ask for in one's spouse?

'One picture,' he had begged. 'One dirty picture. Something for me to look at when you are not with me.' After much deliberation, she had said yes.

He had clicked one picture. And then two more. But then he had felt bad 'owning' her like this, so he had sent them to her. 'I am in them too,' he had said, 'we are both naked, just like the day we were born.'

They had laughed, and because he may have been drunk, instead of sending the pictures to just her, he had sent them to his entire phonebook, to the friends they had in common, and the recruiters who had been considering hiring them both.

Magically, miraculously, Malati forgave him. 'Neel, I know it was a mistake. We can't control who saw what or how they reacted. If they are decent human beings, they deleted the pictures. If they aren't, they didn't, and that's horrid. But either way, you and I can't tell them what to do. Nor can we change what happened. So, please, let's just forget about it.'

He had tried. He had really, really tried. But he hadn't been able to. It had angered him to see Malati brush it aside. How could she? Did she not realize that everyone must have stared at her naked, far-from-perfect body? Surely, they must have laughed at her oversized arms? At the hair curled in her pits and the stretch marks that criss-crossed her belly? Did they laugh imagining his thrusts while riding her? Worse, did they imagine her on top, and him lying there like a weakling, just taking it? It built up inside Neel, this rot of rage, humiliation and something else, something he couldn't name. It thickened like syrup and darkened his insides like poison.

Shortly thereafter, he ended things. 'I hope we can still be friends,' Neel told Malati. 'I hope you understand where I am coming from. I need to be with someone I can be proud of, someone I can be attracted to. I want to marry someone who is proud of herself.' He remembered the way she had looked at him, how her smile had first vanished from her eyes, and how by the end of that week, she too had vanished from Delhi.

Neel fisted his hands and pressed them to his eyes. No, not Malati. Only Misha now. Misha, his wife, his entire world. He rolled to her side of the bed and shook her again. When she groaned, he asked, 'What will help? Will it help if we argue? Will it energize you to write something new?'

Misha mumbled. She yanked at a pillow and put it over her head.

For the rest of the night, they tried to fall back to sleep.

~

Every Friday, Misha visited her parents and Neel worked from home. So, on that particular Friday, when his phone rang, he thought it was someone from his office. Instead, it was Ruhi. It had been three years since her visit, but he recalled her face, body and anecdotes, and the story that they became, thanks to his wife's ministrations.

'Are you two okay?' Ruhi asked. 'I have sent Misha many messages, but she hasn't replied. I got your number from your office.'

'Yes, thanks,' Neel said. 'Misha hasn't been very social.'

'Oh, new book, is it?'

'Something like that.'

'Listen, I don't have a lot of time, but I have a few gifts for you guys. May I drop them off?'

'Of course,' Neel said. 'Please come. I am home.' The faint outline of an idea started taking shape in his mind. 'I know you are busy, but it would really mean so much to us if you stay for dinner.'

When Ruhi said 'yes', Neel vacuumed the apartment, then dashed to the market for a bouquet and white wine. He showered and dressed with care. He put on his most expensive cologne. He stared at his reflection. He wondered if his plan would work as he gathered the ingredients for dinner. He wanted to cook them spaghetti with meatballs.

Ruhi arrived and he poured her a glass of wine. When it was almost time for Misha to return, Neel led her to the kitchen. Just as he had hoped, Ruhi asked if she could help.

When he heard the faint click of Misha's key turning in their door, he nudged closer to Ruhi. He sensed Misha's presence at the mouth of the kitchen, her eyes on their backs, her body rigid at the unexpected sound of their voices and laughs. He kept Ruhi distracted. He let Misha watch them—her husband and her friend—their warm, moist fingers working together, moulding the spiced, ground meat into perfect, delectable rounds.

Ruhi left shortly after dinner. Neel busied himself in cleaning the kitchen and putting away leftovers. For the first time in months, he heard the study door click shut, followed immediately by the staccato click-clack of the keyboard. Neel beamed. His plan had worked. Satisfied, he wiped the counters clean and readied himself for sleep.

When he entered the bedroom, Misha was already there.

'Done already?' Neel looked at her in surprise. 'Usually when you start writing at night you go on for hours.'

Misha closed her eyes. 'Sorry, can we chat about this another time? I am tired.'

'Yes,' Neel said. He turned off the lights and climbed into bed. He had expected Misha to be charged by the evening. Like she used to be whenever they had a fight or disagreement, and she would distil it and pour it into her writing. Neel adjusted his pillow and stared at the ceiling.

The following Friday, Misha was off at her parents again. Neel made a couple of calls. He described what he needed. He specified height and approximate weight. He insisted on a certain kind of attire, shoes, hair length and colour. He suggested a wig. *No, money wasn't an issue. Yes, he was a picky customer. He had discerning taste.*

When the woman arrived, Neel considered her carefully. He liked the peaked cap. He loved the near-perfect wig. He took her to the bedroom he shared with his wife.

A few minutes later, he heard Misha's key turn in the main door. She took off her shoes and approached the bedroom. He sensed her standing at the door, a bag slung over her right shoulder, keys and phone in her left hand. He hoped she was taking it all in, the pilot's uniform discarded on the floor, the cap flung carelessly on the bed. He felt her eyes on his back, at his butt, as it pinched and thrust in rhythm. He heard her footsteps retreat, then the quiet pull of the front door as she shut it behind her and left.

That night, Misha didn't come home.

Before calling her friends, Neel sat with what he had done. Not for the first time since Malati's departure, he offered her yet another silent apology. He had searched for her online, on Facebook, but he hadn't found her. Not that he knew what he would say or do if she popped up somewhere. Would he really apologize? Wouldn't that make things worse? This reliving of the experience? He rubbed the back of his neck as he mulled over questions that crossed his mind frequently. Really, where was Malati these days? What did she do? Where did she live? He imagined her married. He imagined her with children who had the same bright, smiling eyes as her. When he felt his throat closing up, Neel stepped out into the balcony. It had taken him a long time to admit, even to himself, who it was that he had been ashamed of in those leaked photographs, whose skinny arms and thin frame he had been fixated on, whose confidence and sense of self-worth he had envied. And why, on the day of his wedding to Misha, he had promised, no, sworn, that he would always put her first and take care of her, in every way possible.

One after the other, Neel called Misha's friends. He left worried messages on her phone. Close to dawn, he drifted off to sleep on the sofa. When he woke up a few hours later, his neck was tight, his shoulders were numb. But he saw the closed door of the study and heard the tap-tap-tap of the laptop keys charged with fury.

Neel readied himself for the day. He brushed his teeth. He showered. His heart felt both empty and full as he made himself a cup of coffee. Then slowly, systematically, he packed his clothes. He grabbed his pouch of medicines and his travel kit. He slipped off his wedding ring and placed it on his bedside table. He was about to walk out of the bedroom, when he turned to take one final look. He would miss this space. He had been happy here, mostly.

The study door opened and Misha stepped out. Her eyes were red and swollen. She clasped and unclasped her hands. She nodded at his suitcase, as if it was a person needing acknowledgement. 'So . . .?' she asked, not finishing the question.

'You are writing again,' Neel said. 'I am happy.' He picked up the suitcase and came to stand before his wife. This was his final gift to her. His betrayal, the fuel for her writing. His leaving home, the push she needed. She would write another story, he had no doubt, perhaps even a new novel. Would they make it though? As a couple? He didn't know. But for now, he had done what he had to.

'Thank you,' Misha whispered. She knew what he had done. 'Thank you,' she said again, her voice trembling. She stepped aside to let Neel go.

THE READER

Raninagar, Bengal, 1899

Binu, ten years old and newly married, glared at her husband through her veil. There were two reasons for it. Her parents had told her that she was not to take *Devi Bhagwat Purana,* her one and only book, to her new home. She had read it so many times that the pages were as worn as her father's good dhoti, and yet, she had to leave this object of affection behind.

Second, she had hoped her husband, Nabin Choudhury, would be nicer looking than Paritosh Da, her sister Bidhi's husband. But, unlike Paritosh Da who had a head full of hair and an easy smile, Nabin was already balding. Plus, his thin moustache was like the tail of a mouse, and he had a sweaty, disapproving face. For the entirety of their wedding ceremony, he had sat with his lips pressed together, as if a bitter melon had been forced into his mouth. Binu had caught him smiling only once, when Phul Di, his sister, had started ululating.

As far as she could tell, Nabin's only virtue lay in that he wasn't as loud as Paritosh Da. Really, why couldn't one of the elders tell him to be quiet? No one had asked him to go on and on about their English doctor. Or hold forth on how some new English book was better than all of Bankim Babu's novels. Not that Binu knew either Bankim Babu or what constituted novels, but she liked peace and quiet and hoped one of the white-haired men would say, 'Enough now, Paritosh. Let someone else talk.'

As she struggled to sit up straight in her Benarasi sari, Binu reasoned that perhaps Nabin never smiled because he went to college, which meant that he was a serious man. How and when did you become a serious woman? Was it when you married a serious man, or when you became the mother of a serious boy?

Her tears came minutes after they boarded the train, as it slowly, reluctantly, exhaled out of the station she had known her entire life towards the unknown. Binu sniffed into her sari. No one noticed, though the compartment was packed with Nabin's family, friends and relatives. Or maybe they did but thought it best to leave her alone. It is also possible they couldn't tell because her veil came down to her chin, and they thought she was mesmerized by the landmarks speeding by—bamboo trees, tall like the zamindar's henchmen; a dusty hill in the shape of a mushroom; tea stalls packed with customers; flower sellers with marigolds and hibiscus heaped in baskets; a clutch of terracotta temples; and boys milling around and jostling in a school playground.

Soon, the people sitting closest to her, Phul Di and several of Nabin's female cousins, dropped off to sleep. Binu craned her neck this way and that, but she couldn't see Nabin. She leaned her head against the window and tried to memorize the landmarks in the order in which they appeared. She wondered if doing so might be useful if her in-laws ever tired of her and decided to send her away.

Her eyes grew heavy, but Binu didn't want to sleep. She had many questions about Nabin's family. She had overheard her mother telling her sisters that his family was rich. But how rich? Like Paritosh Da's family? Did everyone have their own beds? Would she get one of her own too? On her wedding day, Bidhi had received several saris from her husband's family, and she had sat surrounded by her loot, smug and prim, like an empress. At the very least, Binu decided, if not an empress, she would most definitely enjoy feeling like the princess of a minor kingdom.

She couldn't tell how long they had been in the train when Phul Di called her name. 'Notun Bou, we have arrived. See? This is our station,' Phul Di pointed outside. Binu looked too. This station was bigger and busier than the one in her village. The platform seemed to go on forever.

'Come, Notun Bou, come,' Phul Di urged, helping Binu to her feet. 'Our house isn't far, but today it might take a while. So many people have come here to see you.'

'Why?' Binu asked.

'What do you mean why? To see you, silly! People are curious. They want to know what the new bride looks like.'

Binu nodded to show she understood, but her stomach churned when her feet landed on the platform. She saw hordes of people, mostly women and children, far louder and noisier than anything she had seen before. Were they really there for her? It had rained earlier in the day, and now there were puddles the size of wheels. Binu stumbled. She squinted through her veil as she tried to keep pace with Phul Di. Every face was a blur.

The train journey hadn't been wholly unpleasant. The wide-open windows on both sides had let in a cool breeze. The sticky heat Binu now experienced, however, was unbearable. Her stomach growled. Luckily, no one heard. She hadn't had much to eat all day, had she? If she was home right now, Ma would have handed her a bowl of puffed rice with a pinch of salt, chopped onion and green chili, and a pour of mustard oil, whose pungency would have made her sneeze. The memory of the salt, heat and oil flooded Binu's mouth. She stifled a sob. No one heard it. *Not now, please, not now,* she warned herself. This was neither the time nor place.

Nabin's two-storeyed house stood diagonally across from a Kali temple. A group of women hovered by its entrance, and a cat napped on one of its stone steps. A banyan tree towered over the temple like an oversized umbrella, its streaming branches threatening to root through the walls.

The house itself was staggering, with its high ceilings, arched doors, shuttered windows and wide stairs. There were fruit trees and flower bushes, and a square-shaped courtyard that accommodated more people than Binu had seen in her ten years so far. Nearly everyone Nabin was related to, everyone spilling from one room to another, was older than Binu, and therefore deserving of her obeisance. She lost track of how many times she bent down to touch their feet or take their blessings, their hands pressing into her head, repeating the same set of words over and over again—*may your husband live forever, may you never be a widow, may you be the mother of a hundred sons.*

Until this experience, it hadn't occurred to Binu that feet came in so many sizes and shapes, or that toenails could cover the entire range from clean to rough to gnarly, not unlike the texture of the stone steps leading up to the temple. Her veil slipped a few hundred times, and each time Phul Di set it straight, so that Binu could continue being a decorous bride.

At dusk, she accompanied the women to the Kali temple. A hundred conches went off, and Binu felt a dam break inside her, memories swirling like a flood. She remembered early morning dips in the river with Ma, eating mango pickles with Bidhi before she got married, and reading and rereading her favourite story from the *Devi Bhagwat Purana*, the one about the epic battle between Kali and the demon Raktabīja.

Baba had always told her that the book was hers. And yet, the night before her wedding, he had changed his mind. 'Don't take it with you, Binu. Who knows how your new family would react?' Her mother had agreed. 'Listen to your father,' she had said, nodding firmly. 'Nabin might not want a wife with too many ideas.'

The memory of her mother's voice brought a fresh flood of tears, and this time, Binu couldn't help it. She sobbed and a hush descended on the women around her. Phul Di burst into a peal of laughter. It was not unkind though.

Her mother-in-law, who had mostly been quiet thus far, drew Binu close. She stroked her head. 'It will be all right. We all have to go through this. You will be fine.'

Binu wiped her face, but the tears wouldn't stop.

She caught a glimpse of Nabin when they were back inside the house. He was leaning against one of the courtyard pillars, talking to a cousin. He, too, saw Binu, and his face clenched. He said something to his companion, and although she was too far away to hear him, from the way he drew his eyebrows together, it was clear he had not said anything nice.

Did Nabin never smile, Binu thought irritably. He had had to leave his home only for one day, that too for this wedding. Now they were back, but she didn't know when she would ever see hers again. Why was *he* in a sour mood? What had he lost?

When it was night, a few of the women, including Phul Di and her mother-in-law, led Binu to a large room. An exquisite marble-topped table stood in the corner, next to a heavy wooden chair. Two of the four walls were crammed with pictures of gods and goddesses, the third held a clock nearly as tall as Binu, and the fourth held framed pictures and certificates of Nabin's late grandfather. A bed, the size of her parents' entire house, took up space in the centre.

'Is this where I will sleep?' Binu asked. She couldn't help herself. Surely, this bed was the biggest thing in all of Bengal. Her eyes shone with amazement. She knew she wasn't old enough to share a bed with Nabin. That would happen a few years later, and there was no need to think about it now. If only she could show this bed to Bidhi.

The women in the room doubled with laughter. Binu joined in, though she had no idea what had caused this mirth.

'Yes, and no,' her mother-in-law said, a smile stuck on the corners of her lips. 'You will share this bed with Thakuma, Nabin's grandmother.'

Binu felt glad that Bidhi was not around to see her disappointed face.

Just then, two maids brought in Binu's trunk, and following her mother-in-law's instructions, pulled it open. The thin metal bangles on their wrists jangled as they began heaving and hauling items out of it. Binu felt herself shrink. Was this supposed to happen? Wasn't this her trunk? Was she supposed to intervene or offer help?

They arranged the modest saris her parents had bought her on the bed. Next to it, they placed the two small bags of jewellery and a handful of other boxes and knick-knacks they had sent her to help settle in her new home. Finally, one of the maids pulled out what Binu had snuck into the trunk at the last minute.

It was a book. The *Devi Bhagwat Purana*.

Phul Di grabbed the book with amazement. She held it up to Binu's face. 'Child, do you know how to read?'

Binu froze. 'Yes,' she said in a small voice. She had disobeyed her parents. She had shoved in the book when they weren't looking and now her rotten deed was for everyone to see.

'Your new daughter-in-law is an educated lady, Ma,' Phul Di squealed. 'Any day now she will become a professor.'

This ensued even more laughter and hilarity. Binu joined in again, though she didn't know what a professor was.

That night, Binu slept poorly. The room was too big, as was the house, and unfamiliar sounds could be heard through the walls. Were those rats she was hearing? Who was walking up and down the corridor? Could someone have scaled the boundary wall? Maybe he was hiding outside this room. Bidhi said ghosts weren't real, but what did she know? What if this house was haunted?

Binu switched sides, but the bed remained uncomfortable. It was too firm and hurt her back. Fortunately, her restlessness didn't wake Thakuma. She snored through the night, like thunder clapping against the sky. By the time Binu managed to sleep, the birds were out and about.

~

A week later, on a hot afternoon when everyone else was napping, Binu discovered the library. By then, the house had quieted down; the relatives who had arrived for the wedding had left. Binu had never known a house as large as this. There were separate spaces for men and women. The cooking and sleeping sections, pressed against the back of the courtyard, were at a significant distance from the main entrance and the drawing rooms.

She had never once stepped inside the men's rooms. What exactly happened there besides long conversations and arguments over cards, food and the coarse breath of tobacco? She was halfway through the long corridor connecting the two ends of the house when she squatted and unclasped her tinkling anklets. She hooked one to the other and tucked the long chain round and round the bun at the back of her neck.

The first room was disappointing. It contained sacks of grains and lentils, and a shelf lined with cloth-bound ledgers. The solitary window hadn't been opened recently and the room held a distinct earthy-burlap smell. The adjoining room, containing various tools and equipment, was a lot less interesting than the first, although Binu couldn't tell what they were used for. The third room had large, airy windows that went all the way to the ceiling. Adjoining the walls were several chairs, thick, floor cushions and oblong pillows against which to rest one's back. The room smelled clean, but a lingering scent of food and tobacco also clung to every surface. So, this is where the men gathered to talk and smoke, and from where her father-in-law's gruff voice carried all the way to the courtyard.

But it was the fourth room that took Binu's breath away. When she pushed open the heavy doors and entered, her knees nearly buckled and brought her to the floor. She gasped. What was this impossibly beautiful room? She had never seen anything like it. There were books everywhere, from the shelves that started close to the floor and went up to the ceiling, to stacks upon stacks on the desk and matching chair, piled in upright columns throughout the room and on windowsills. She had no idea so many books existed in the world. Who wrote them? Who read them? Where did they come from?

Binu tiptoed to the shelf closest to her. She reached out with her finger and stroked the spine of a heavy, cloth-bound book. She couldn't read what it said. She assumed it was either in English or Sanskrit, two languages her father-in-law spoke fluently she had been told. Her fingers trailed along, gently skimming the spines of the other books. She could read the titles of the ones in Bangla. A few contained pictures. Some had gold lettering on their spines. Binu thought the books looked distinguished and dignified, like magistrates and dignitaries out for a stroll—nothing like the three beat-up books her father owned.

The brass-inlaid desk bore an ornamental sculpture of an elephant, complete with a mahout and howdah. She tried to lift it, but then decided against it. The elephant continued to hold down a thick sheaf of papers. Of the many books on the desk, only one was in Bangla. Binu picked it up with reverence. She opened it to the first page.

It was a dictionary. She had heard of them but never seen one. Rows and rows of words. Who knew all these words? Did anyone ever feel like making up new ones? The dictionary was heavy and Binu's arms soon got tired. She could never have imagined that a single book could weigh so much. She set it down and was still flipping through the pages when something fell out and landed at her feet.

It was a picture of an unsmiling woman. Young and white, she held a clutch of flowers with skinny, pointed petals. Her collar and sleeves were lined with delicate lace and her long, voluminous dress was the colour of night. Though her eyes looked right at you, you couldn't tell what she was thinking. But she seemed unafraid and extremely sure of herself.

A strange thought occurred to Binu. What if this white woman wasn't white? What if she was yet another version of Kali and this picture was taken minutes after she vanquished Raktabīja, an achievement for which someone presented her with flowers.

Was this Nabin's book? Was the woman someone he had hoped to marry? English, unafraid to look him in the eye? Granted, she had seen him only a handful of times since the day of their wedding, but not once had he looked happy. If anything, he had looked angry every time.

'What are you doing here?' a voice boomed from the door.

Binu whipped around. The photograph was still in her hand, and in her haste, she had forgotten to pull her sari all the way so it could cover her head.

It was Nabin.

His eyes were cold and hard, and a line of sweat beaded his upper lip. 'What are you doing here?'

Binu stammered, 'I . . . I . . .'

Nabin's words cut in before she could form her sentence. 'Who gave you permission to go through my things? The library is out of bounds for children.'

Tears sprang into Binu's eyes. She didn't like the way Nabin said 'children', like it was a curse or an insult. She dropped her gaze; her tears turned the floor blurry, but she wasn't going to give Nabin the satisfaction of seeing how deeply his words had wounded her. She put the photograph back on the desk, skirted around him carefully so as to avoid any contact and dashed out of that most perfect room to return to the safety of her own.

Thankfully, no one had noticed her absence. Thakuma was still in the middle of her nap. But for the remainder of the day, Binu's mind played and replayed the only exchange she had thus far with her husband. At some point, though, she stopped feeling sorry for herself. She got angry. 'Is this how any of the goddesses of *Devi Bhagwat Purana* would have behaved? At the sight of the demon, would Kali have broken into tears? Forget the goddesses. What about that Englishwoman in the photograph? She would have stood her ground.'

A week later, Nabin left for Calcutta. He still had courses to complete before he could get his degree. At the hour of his departure, his mother wept as if he was moments from being conscripted into the army. The family walked together to the Kali temple, where Nabin was anointed with dots of vermilion and sandalwood by the head priest and fed a dollop of yoghurt by his mother. He touched his father's feet, then his mother's. He even said something mildly teasing to Phul Di. She, too, was leaving that day to return to the home she shared with her husband, children and in-laws.

But Nabin neither looked at Binu nor said a word to her. Why would he? Who was she but a child who had gone through his things without permission and ran away at the first sign of trouble?

That evening, when the men sat down to eat, Nabin's spot remained empty. Did that Englishwoman cook Bengali food, Binu wondered. She felt a twinge of something—jealousy or envy or irritation—she couldn't tell. She wished she could talk to someone. How would her own mother have handled this situation? Binu couldn't be sure.

A few days later, when the house was as quiet as the Kali temple at night, Binu stole into her favourite room again. She shut the heavy doors behind her. She had learned the right name for this room. Lib-ra-ry. She had heard her father-in-law call it that.

The room was just as she remembered. Quiet, serious and beautiful, and the books themselves pristine on their shelves. Only one item was different. The dictionary had left the premises, and with it, the picture of the Englishwoman. Binu pressed her ear to the door. No one was coming, and the adjoining rooms, the long corridor and the square courtyard were like the people of this house during the afternoon, deep in sleep.

Binu pulled out a book whose title she could read from its spine. *Kapalkundala.* She crept under the massive desk and arranged herself on the cool, mosaic floor. Thus hidden from the world, she opened her contraband. Then, with a happy sigh, she began to read.

Every week, Nabin wrote to his family from Calcutta. The letters were short but full of details about his classes (too much literature, too little logic) and his professors, a mix of Indians and Englishmen. Nabin's father would gather the entire family in the courtyard and read the letters out loud. Every time an Englishman's name was mentioned, his voice took on a more gruff and important-sounding edge. Nabin always ended with assurances that he was eating at regular mealtimes, going out for walks every evening by the Ganges, and only being friends with boys from decent families. He always inquired about his parents, siblings and Thakuma, sometimes even sundry neighbours and other relatives, but not once did he mention Binu.

Was this what it meant to be a wife? To be this invisible? What did he do during the hours in the day when he was not being a student or spending time with his friends from decent families? Did he spend it with *her,* the bold-faced Englishwoman?

Three months later, Nabin returned home for a holiday. On the first night, his mother cooked and fed him a feast. Five kinds of fried vegetables, lentil stew, two vegetable curries, three types of fish cooked three different ways, a slow-cooked mutton, mango and tamarind chutney, an array of his favourite sweets and the best-quality rice there was in the market.

From a spot inside the kitchen, Binu watched Nabin as he ate. No light fell on her face, the lanterns faced the clay oven and the pots and pans filled with food. Nabin smiled at his mother, then laughed at something his father said. He told Thakuma that she could go to sleep and promised her that he would eat properly even without her supervision.

Twice, Binu was instructed to step out by her mother-in-law—the first time to bring out the salt, and after that, to serve the chutney. Not once did Nabin glance in her direction. Did he know who she was? Did he recognize her?

The following afternoon, Binu waited impatiently for Thakuma's snores. She tossed and turned, adjusted and readjusted her pillow, but the combination of humidity and the mustard-heavy fish curry they had had for lunch kept her awake. She lay on her back and stared at the ceiling. It wasn't a terrible life per se, she thought for the hundredth time. Her in-laws were nice enough, but no one really had anything to say to her. It was one quiet day after another.

Twice every day, at dawn and dusk, she accompanied the older women to the Kali temple. At various hours, she was summoned into the kitchen to help out. She now knew how to pickle lemons, fry fish without coughing her lungs out, what spices to add in what order while cooking dal. Outside of the kitchen, she had learned how to mend clothes and embroider flowers. But if it wasn't for the library, and the fourteen books she had read thus far, she would have had a hard time telling one day apart from the next.

At the sound of the first deep snore, Binu bolted from the bed. She had paid so many visits to that forbidden part of the house by now that she could do it with her eyes closed. She had it down to the last second and knew how long it took between her mother-in-law's calls and her father-in-law's footsteps for her to emerge from her spot under the desk, return the book to its proper shelf, open the door without a single creak and bolt towards the kitchen. She had had two close calls but neither was so jarring nor frightening as to make her stop.

She entered the library and closed the heavy doors behind her. But then she stopped. The room felt different. Fresh stacks of books stood rigid on the desk, like soldiers awaiting marching orders. The chair was askew, someone had brought in a floor cushion from the drawing room next door, and despite the windows being open, a scent of tobacco and soap layered the air.

Binu's hands shook. She had forgotten Nabin was home. In her desperation to get here, she had forgotten that he would be here for a week or so. She was about to dash out when something on the desk caught her eye. It was the dictionary again, taking up most of the room, like it owned everything.

Binu drew her breath sharply. Slowly, carefully, so as to not disturb the rest of the books, she pulled the dictionary towards herself. This time too, she let the heavy book open naturally to a page, and there she was, the Englishwoman, her gaze steady, her skin white as milk.

Anger shot through Binu's core. Did Nabin think he was so handsome that he deserved an Englishwoman? Was he even half as handsome as Paritosh Da? No. He had hardly any hair left. He deserved Binu, nothing or no one more. A white woman? Absolutely not. Who did he think he was?

Binu glared at the photograph. This woman, right here, was what had fuelled his misplaced confidence. If she was gone, he would return to his senses. Only by destroying her would she be able to save him. Surely, as his wife, this was her duty.

Binu tightened her grip on the photograph and tore it into two roughly equal halves. Not satisfied, she kept at it. She pulled apart the pieces until the picture was reduced to a crumbly, fluttering mess.

The doors swung open and there stood Nabin, a book in his hands. Did he also have a habit of reading in the afternoons?

When he saw Binu, Nabin looked just as surprised. Clearly, she wasn't the only one who had forgotten about the existence of the other.

'What on earth do you think you are doing?' Nabin asked, storming inside. 'Haven't I told you never to come here?' He wasn't as loud or gruff-sounding as his father, and yet, somehow, he seemed more intimidating.

Binu pursed her lips. She felt tears form at the corners of her eyes, but she stood firm. She had done what needed to be done. If Nabin could refuse to acknowledge her, very well, she would do the same. She would not answer his questions.

'Did I not tell you that you are not allowed here?' Nabin demanded. 'I don't want you to pull out pages from these books and turn them into boats or kites or something nonsensical. These aren't playthings.'

A sound, like crying, escaped Binu's throat. She thought of Kali in her temple, just two walls away from where she stood. She thought of the fierce goddesses of her book, tucked away in her trunk, a quick run from this room. She imagined them huddled around her, bolstering her, giving her all their strength. 'Don't give in, Binu,' they whispered. Binu squared her shoulders. No, she would not run away this time.

Nabin sighed. He went around the desk, straightened the chair and sat down. 'Really, why are you here? My father will be furious if he finds out.'

'But how will he find out? He naps right until the shadow of the banyan tree touches the west wall of the Kali temple,' Binu blurted.

'What?'

'What am I to do when everyone sleeps in the afternoon? When no one will talk to me? When there is *Kapalkundala* here, and, and . . .' Binu cried, the words dying in her mouth at the sight of Nabin's startled face.

'What did you say? *Kapalkundala*?'

Binu heard the incredulity in Nabin's voice. What would her mother say if she saw her now, defying her college-going husband, the man she was duty-bound to honour for seven lifetimes? But Binu couldn't be quieted.

'Who is she?' Binu demanded.

'Who is who?'

'The Englishwoman.'

'The Englishwoman?'

'The Englishwoman in the picture.' Binu held up her hands, cupped around the dregs of what once was a photograph.

Nabin's eyes widened. 'Oh, her. What happened here?' When Binu didn't answer but continued to look mutinous, he said, 'I don't know who she is. I think she is an actress. I found the picture on the floor of my university library. I didn't know whose it was, so I put it inside my book.' He added sheepishly. 'She is . . . was . . . beautiful, wasn't she? But really, I don't know her.' His tone was gentler this time.

Binu shifted on her feet. 'I will stop coming here,' she said.

Nabin was quiet for a moment. Then he spoke. 'Do you know,' he hesitated, 'that I find this distasteful?'

Binu reddened. 'I do. I won't come here again,' she repeated.

'No, no, not this, not your visits to the library. *This*,' Nabin indicated the space between the two of them. 'This. This marriage between you, a child, and me, a fully grown man. This isn't right. This doesn't happen everywhere. It shouldn't happen here, not in this day and age. You should be a lot older. You should have a say.'

Binu blinked. She didn't understand this turn the conversation had taken or where it was headed.

'I want you to know that I am in no rush to be your husband,' Nabin said. He rose from the chair and briskly walked out of the room.

Binu stood, unmoving, the dictionary flat on the desk and the photograph still cupped in her palms. Was Nabin about to complain to his parents about her? Were they going to send her away? As much as she wanted to see her parents, Binu knew that that would be terrible. They wouldn't be able to bear the shame. Wives packed off to their parents' home were never called back.

That night, after Thakuma had gone off to sleep, Binu picked up her book again. It had been a long time since she had turned those pages. She felt comforted by the heft of the book in her hands, but in spite of her efforts, she struggled to concentrate on the words. They swam, in this direction and that, the room quiet except for the noises she had grown accustomed to, the wind whistling through the trees outside, and inside, the creaks of the house and the snores of Thakuma.

A noise, like a small cough, made Binu sit up. She adjusted the flame of the lantern. No, she had not imagined it. Someone was out there and this person's long shadow was cast upon the door. The footsteps drew closer. It was Nabin.

She couldn't read his expression. Was he about to deliver his punishment? Had he come to order her to pack her clothes and leave? Was someone going to take her home or would she have to board the train by herself? Binu glanced at the sleeping form of Thakuma. The old lady liked her enough, but could she be expected to intercede?

Nabin drew closer. He didn't say anything. Was Binu expected to get up from the bed? Was she supposed to say something? Offer him food or water? Touch his feet? Her heart pounding, Binu waited.

Nabin took off his sandals and sat beside her. Binu's limbs turned to stone. He was so close that he could slap her if he wanted. His hands looked smooth, but no doubt there was strength in them. He reached over and adjusted the lantern. The flame grew softer, the room shrank in size, and Binu thought, 'Any moment now.' She closed her eyes.

She felt Nabin place something heavy in her lap. It was big and boxy. Binu still didn't open her eyes. Then she felt his hands on hers and her throat tightened. He placed her hands on the object.

'Look,' Nabin whispered. 'Binu, open your eyes.'

Binu obeyed. He knew her name. She wasn't sure why it surprised her, but it did. In a good way.

'It's yours,' Nabin said. 'And there will be many more in the future. You just keep reading.'

It was a book.

It had a navy blue dust jacket and gold letters on the cover and the spine. Binu looked up in surprise, her mouth rounding in a perfect circle. Nabin's face broke into a smile, and for the first time since she had seen him on the day of their wedding, it was a smile just for her.

And then, just as quickly as he had appeared, Nabin was gone.

Binu whispered the title of the book. *Devi Chaudhurani.* It was by the same author who had written *Kapalkundala.* Bankim Chandra Chattopadhyay. Paritosh Da had made fun of him at her wedding. All Paritosh Da had was a nice face. He had probably seen the size of the book and set it aside.

Binu gently opened the book to the first page. She had already read it, of course, from the library, but only once. There were hundreds and hundreds of times she could, and would, read it again. No one had ever gifted her a book. No one had told her to keep reading, that there were more books coming. From somewhere inside her, Binu heard her mother's warning. *What if Nabin doesn't want a wife with too many ideas?*

He had scrawled his name on the first page. Binu ran her fingers over it and let her mother's words grow faint. *But he does, Ma,* she whispered, and began reading.

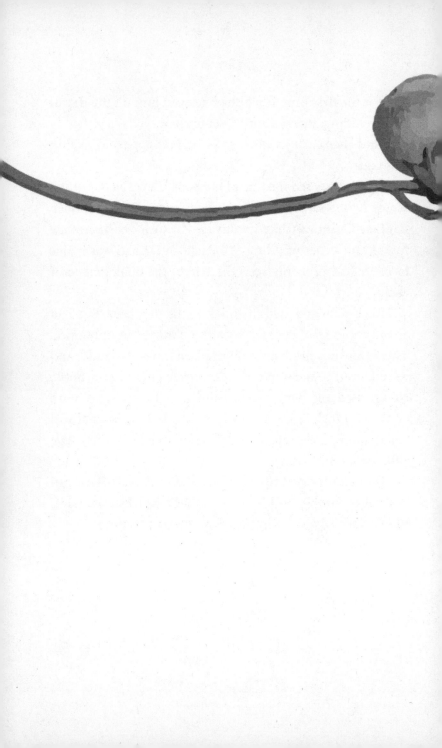

MISS
JOSEPHINE

When Miss Josephine died, we all cried like we had lost our mothers. But Miss Josephine looked nothing like our mothers. She was neither brown nor young; she did not wear cotton saris or nylon salwar-kameezes. Miss Josephine was old and white, her face the texture of beaten leather, her hair a nest of grey. Her skin turned a vivid red in the sun, as if she had been held against her wishes and someone had struck angry welts on her body. That's why our mothers said, 'God never intended for Miss Josephine to be in India.'

But we, her fan club, vehemently disagreed. Because without Miss Josephine, our childhood wouldn't have tasted very good. It would have been as unremarkable as that of kids in neighbourhoods that didn't have an old, white lady baker of their own. It was Miss Josephine's black forest cake that we ate on our birthdays, the leftovers of her pastries that we nibbled on when our mothers hosted kitty parties, and her rum cakes and fruit pies that marked our Christmases and New Years. Without Miss Josephine, how would we have ever learned to appreciate an apple strudel or its flaky crust? Her foods nourished us as much as our mothers' milk, but unlike our mothers, Miss Josephine rarely smiled and never once asked about our well-being. What she lacked in motherly love, she more than made up with her creations—rich, gooey and saturated with sugar.

No one quite knew when Miss Josephine had first moved into the corner house. She was already there when our mothers arrived, one after the other, as blushing brides, eager and excited to start this new chapter of their lives. Of course, the corner house wasn't really a house. It had been built to function as an annexe, but the landlord had rented it out to make some extra money on the side.

From the outside, it was unimpressive to say the least. It was blotchy and grey, the colour of spit. It was box-shaped with plain brown windows on all four sides. Despite multiple attempts and our best efforts, we could never see through the windows. Miss Josephine kept them covered with heavy curtains, and if she ever washed and changed them, she surely did so in the middle of the night with the lights turned off. Whenever any of her customers found out where she lived, they always seemed shocked that the maker of such divine creations, an artist in her own right, could exist, day after day, in something so utterly devoid of colour and character. No one ever saw the inside of her house because in all the years she lived on our street, Miss Josephine never invited anyone.

When we asked our mothers why, they came up with a variety of explanations, some more creative than others—perhaps Miss Josephine kept her secret recipes inside a locked cabinet that she didn't want to show the world, perhaps she was embarrassed that brown people lived in bigger homes than hers, perhaps she liked the peace and quiet for prayer and meditation purposes, or maybe because one of her family members was a notorious serial killer and she had his life-size poster on a wall. Their answers never satisfied us, and so Miss Josephine's house remained a mystery. The only evidence of her artistry lay in the neatly trimmed row of grass surrounding the annexe. She kept it clean and perfect, as if in readiness of a military-grade inspection.

One summer, we came up with an innovative plan to peek inside her home. As soon as Miss Josephine returned from the bakery, we decided to march over with a big bowl of turmeric paste (that we told her was from our mothers), so that she could put it on her skin and soothe herself. We would knock loudly on her door and wait. She would open it a crack and poke her head out, her beady blue eyes watchful, as if for monsters, her sparse eyebrows pinched and her thick chin quivering slightly. We would breathe in the mixed smells coming from within—washing soap, cabbage, vanilla—but could never tell if she was genuinely scared or hamming it up for our benefit. Her frightened face only made us uncomfortable, and after a week of attempts, we gave up. Needless to say, not once did she thank us for the turmeric paste, nor did she invite us in.

Miss Josephine dressed the same every day. She wore large, full-sleeved blouses in black or grey and thick skirts that came down to her calves. She didn't own any jewellery except for a slim, silver-dial watch with a black strap, which may have fit her once but was now clamped on her left wrist like the jaws of a shark. Her sagging skin, speckled with red and brown freckles, stretched uncomfortably over her hands and face as if they couldn't contain her weight any more. Her ankles were as fat as trees and we joked that she must have to sleep with her shoes on—the sturdy, black leather ones so tight that we were sure she could not pry them off, and yet, their buckles shone as if she polished them every night.

Our mothers scolded us whenever they caught us giggling over Miss Josephine. They told us to leave her alone because, clearly, that's what the old lady wanted. Plus, she never troubled anyone. But often, our mothers too succumbed to the same temptation, and we would hear them chuckling over how little Miss Josephine had changed since the time each of them had first arrived in the neighbourhood. 'She must have been born old,' was everyone's conclusion.

Sometimes, our mothers would worry about Miss Josephine too. 'She is getting on in her years,' they would say. 'Wonder if she has any family anywhere.' And then they would add, 'She really should be a little more forthright and tell us about herself. Who will run around if something happens? Hospital, doctors, medicines—who will shoulder that responsibility? Of course, we will help. We are good, decent people here. But still, family is family.' Were our mothers genuinely concerned? Or did they know how to make excuses in advance?

In spite of god knows how many decades in this country, Miss Josephine only spoke English. She didn't sound English though; we knew what English English was like. We had watched enough episodes of *Yes, Prime Minister* and *Mind Your Language*. But every time we asked her where she was from, Miss Josephine shooed us away.

Dipti, taller and often smarter than the rest of us, and our self-proclaimed leader because she was two whole years older, insisted that Miss Josephine sounded like she could be from Austria. We had no choice but to take her word because, thanks to her diplomat father, Dipti had spent three months in Austria and now considered herself the last word on all things European.

The year Miss Josephine retired from the bakery, an American ice-cream shop opened across the street. Miss Josephine continued to sell some of her specialities from home, provided we remembered to put in a request the night before. More often than not, we forgot, which was just as well. By then we were almost twelve and desserts stopped mattering as much. Or they did but we knew how to suppress our greed than to give in like gluttons.

The ice-cream shop offered a whole new world, filled with unusual flavours and exciting, infinite possibilities. But the biggest temptation it offered was the high school boys from Don Bosco who stopped there every evening after soccer practice.

We watched them from the corners of our eyes. Sweaty from practice, they smelled of dirt, dust, grass and something else. They took up the entire corner table, pulling in chairs noisily as if they owned the place. They looked at us appraisingly, and their gaze heated something underneath our skin. Sometimes they smiled at us, though to them we were probably nothing more than little girls. But we didn't *feel* like little girls. So, we watched them—those toned arms, the sweat pearling against their skin, the way they licked their mouths and wiped their chins.

Miss Josephine died the year most of us turned thirteen. It was her landlord who discovered her. He had stopped by, puzzled that she was two days late in paying her rent. Apparently, that had never happened in the twenty-nine years she had been his tenant. When he broke open the door, he found her in bed. The doctor declared that she had died in her sleep. Heart failure. Mostly painless. Like she had been throughout her life, in death too, Miss Josephine was quiet and unobtrusive. She didn't scream or shout or in any way inconvenience the people who lived around her.

We were at school when it happened, probably planning yet another trip to the ice-cream shop in the evening, to tease both our taste buds and our eyes. We heard it in the afternoon, when the school bus dropped us home and our mothers rushed to us with the news.

By then, the landlord's servants had removed her body. With the doors and windows wide open, her house resembled a demolished cake, its innards spilled out for everyone to witness its humiliation. When the landlord saw us approaching, he gave us a wan smile and said we were free to pick up anything we thought had sentimental value before he sent in the servants to clean. He warned us to not be disappointed though— as far as he could tell, Miss Josephine owned nothing of value.

His permission seemed so outrageous and unbelievable that for a few moments we forgot Miss Josephine was dead. We ran all the way, pushing and shoving each other to be the first to enter this Aladdin's cave that had so far been denied to us. Our mothers followed right behind, walking as quickly as their dignity would allow. We came to an abrupt stop at the door, as if any moment now Miss

Josephine would emerge and shoo us away. But that didn't happen. When we remembered our reason for being there, fresh tears pricked our eyes.

We entered a room lit resentfully by the last rays of a setting sun. It revealed a plain cement floor and patchy grey walls in need of repair. The outlines against the windows clearly showed where the thick, heavy curtains had once been. In spite of the open windows and sunshine, the house smelled faintly of cabbage and vanilla. Dipti's mother coughed loudly and clamped the end of her pallu to her nose as if she would be the next one to drop dead if she wasn't too careful. Only her eyes were visible above her sari-face mask, and she looked like an overgrown owl, round-eyed and watchful.

The drawing room led directly into the kitchen and onto the bedroom and bathroom on the left. We trooped into the kitchen, which had an old but functional gas stove, nothing even remotely fancy. The shelves tacked to the walls contained an assortment of overused pots, baking pans, measuring cups and spoons. Someone reminded Dipti of how she had once claimed that Miss Josephine had offered to teach her how to make the most perfect apple strudels. We laughed as Dipti's cheeks coloured at the memory of her tall tale. After all, we didn't get too many opportunities to prove she wasn't that much better than us. Really, how could she have thought we would believe her fantastic story?

A few books on baking were propped against the kitchen counter and our mothers advanced towards them like a mob. We left them there and entered the bedroom, which was as sparse as the rest of the house. It, too, had a distinct smell, a combination of detergent and old clothes. The single bed had already been stripped bare of sheets and now held two worn pillows and a thin mattress, stained yellow with age. A modest-sized closet held Miss Josephine's entire array of eight full-sleeved cotton dresses and skirts, and three bulky sweaters in black, brown and navy. At the sight of her familiar dresses, a few in our group started sobbing. We huddled around to comfort them and didn't notice when Dipti moved past us towards the bookshelf beside Miss Josephine's bed.

'What's this?' she cried.

We ran to her, our gaze following the direction of her finger.

All five shelves were filled with identical notebooks, the kinds we used in school, inexpensive and with ruled pages inside. Miss Josephine had numbered them all. There were forty-one of them, their years jotted and taped to the spines.

Greedily, Dipti pulled down the diary marked 'I'. A hush descended into the room as we crowded around her. She opened the first page. We read the date—1 January 1948—and recognized the neat, spindly letters. They were Miss Josephine's, all right. We had seen her write down orders at the bakery and at home; we had read her many receipts. The page in the notebook, however, contained four word repeated s over and over. At least we assumed they were four words. We recognized the letters and sounded them out, but strung like that they made no sense. Nothing was capitalized or punctuated. Just a string of letters repeated again and again—*ich wusste nicht herschel. ich wusste nicht herschel. ich wusste nicht herschel. ich wusste nicht herschel. ich wusste nicht herschel. I.C.H.W.U.S.S.T.E.N.I.C.H.T.H.E.R.S.C.H.E.L.*

Dipti turned the page. It was the same four words again. Unpronounceable. Unfathomable. The notebook switched hands, but irrespective of who tried and how many times, the letters didn't make any sense. Dipti looked stumped too, which was its own reward in some ways.

Impatiently and with arms outstretched like we were meeting long-lost relatives, we pulled down the remaining diaries. All forty-one of them. We propped against chairs, spread ourselves on the floor, each of us grabbing a few and checking them meticulously—the first page, then the last, and then to make sure, opening it randomly in the middle and zipping through a few more.

It didn't matter what year we picked or which diary. They were exactly the same. We repeated it like a chant until we had memorized the letters. Our mothers took turns too, but one by one they failed as well. We hoped our fathers would fare better.

Suddenly, there was a tearing sound. It was Dipti. She had ripped out one of the pages from Miss Josephine's last diary. For a moment, everyone froze. We watched Dipti hold up the page in her right hand, like a triumphant heroine posing with her prize. She closed the diary with a *thwup* sound and slid it back with the others. She surveyed our mutinous expressions and shrugged. 'What?' she asked.

A volley of protests rained down on her—'How could you?', 'Why did you tear the page?', 'What will happen now?', 'How dare you?', 'Have you no shame?'

Dipti snarled. 'Stop overreacting! It's just one page. It's not like Miss Josephine will rise from the dead to seek revenge.'

Hushed and reprimanded, a few of us moved to the other side of the bed to investigate her dresser. The top drawer contained a few pieces of underwear and socks, clean but balled up, as if mourning the loss of their mistress. The bottom drawer contained a ration card, a gift certificate from a grocery store and two letters from satisfied customers. No pictures or maps anywhere. No record of who Miss Josephine may once have been.

Her silver watch sat on top of the dresser. Like everything else we had seen so far, this too was two steps away from absolute ruin. There were scratches on the glass dial. When we flipped it, we saw an engraving on the back. But it had been so badly damaged that we couldn't tell if it was a bird or an animal, or perhaps a human face. We ran our fingers over it, hoping for clues. But the difference between this item and the others was that someone, presumably Miss Josephine herself, had worked hard to destroy the engraving.

Calmly, Dipti pocketed the watch, and once again, a minor scuffle broke out. Truth be told, none of us really wanted to take it home. What if it was now possessed by Miss Josephine's ghost? But we did want to hold it for a little while longer.

Contrary to our hope and belief, when we took the mysterious words home, our fathers were of no help at all. Dipti telephoned her father that night since she claimed he spoke two European languages. But nothing came of that either.

To her credit, Dipti did not give up. So what if Miss Josephine had not divulged her apple strudel recipe? Dipti was determined to extract this one secret out of her. She promised that she wouldn't rest until she solved this mystery. She took the letters to school the next day and showed them to our English teacher. Miss Roy wasn't of any help either, but she did give the terrific suggestion of taking the letters over to the language experts at the college library. We wanted to go too, but our mothers would not have allowed the long trip. Dipti, however, was unstoppable. She waited until the weekend and half-biked, half-bussed her way to the library, while we waited at home, anxious for answers.

Dipti didn't return with anything really useful. Apparently, the first three words meant 'I did not know' in German, and the fourth, 'Herschel', was a man's name. All these years, Miss Josephine had been writing 'I did not know Herschel' over and over again. Did she mean she did not know a Herschel? Or was it to be read as 'I did not know, Herschel.' Was it a confession? Or an explanation? No one had a clue.

Two weeks later, an excited Dipti rounded us up. She had taken Miss Josephine's silver watch to the local watchmaker for cleaning, and he had telephoned to say it was ready to be picked up. We set out for the shop immediately. Although we were a group of almost-teenage girls, our collective barging into his small store quickly cleared it of his other customers. The watchmaker, a man easily in his fifties, and with sideburns the size of squirrels, considered us irritably. Shaking his head, he pulled out the watch. We gathered around his glass table, fogging it up with our breath. He took his time, as if he knew how important this was for us and he wanted to milk his moment of glory for as long as he could.

When he finally flipped over the watch and showed us the cleaned back, we gasped. The cleaning had not taken off the scratches. But now, the metal showed the clear outline of an eagle. Its head was pointed to the left, and the wings, proud and precise, were spread apart gloriously. We recognized it immediately from our history books, from the chapter dedicated to the Second World War.

But that was not all. The watchmaker licked his lips. Then, with the flair of a wizard about to show off his greatest trick, he removed the hinged back of the watch and handed Dipti an eyeglass. 'Go on,' he said.

Dipti put the glass to her eye. She leaned in for a closer look and her head jerked up.

'What is it?' we asked. 'What do you see?'

'Herschel,' Dipti said, handing the eyeglass to the nearest girl. 'Yes, Herschel. Finally.'

She was right. There it was. The name Herschel engraved in tiny letters and next to it, the year 1944.

We walked back home slowly, our minds in a whirl, questions running in an endless loop. Was Miss Josephine a war criminal? Was she German? Austrian? A soldier? Or a guard, secretary, or nurse. Perhaps she was a baker who killed people by feeding them poisoned bread? Who was Herschel? What was she saying to him? Was she apologizing? What happened to her family? When did she arrive in India? And why did she choose to live in our mid-sized city with few things to compare it to Europe? If she didn't want to be reminded of that time in her life, why did she keep the watch? Why didn't she destroy it? Why did she wear it every day of her life? Could it be that a small part of her was actually proud of the work she had done, of the role she may have played? Or was wearing this last artefact of Herschel a punishment for what she may have done?

Finally, Dipti voiced what we had all been thinking. 'Miss Josephine may have been a Nazi. I think she wanted Herschel to forgive her.' When she saw our stricken faces, Dipti softened her tone. 'There is no point in trying to understand why she did what she did. People do stupid things all the time.'

We nodded. We decided never to talk about Miss Josephine again. We weren't going to let a war criminal have that kind of power over us any more. We were going to look forward to our future and not cling on to childhood memories out of sentimentality.

The days turned into months and the boys of Don Bosco became more of a reality. We grew up from little girls to young women who could no longer be ignored. As expected, Dipti was the first one among us to get a boyfriend—a smart, studious fellow who also played soccer. The rest of didn't lag too far behind. Soon, the ice-cream shop became the go-to spot for group dates. But as the years progressed, we outgrew it too and opted instead for restaurants and pubs. Some of us stayed on in the same city, while others migrated to foreign shores. We got ourselves degrees, jobs, nice apartments, pets and a fiancé or two.

Years later, we returned to our neighbourhood to attend the first wedding in our group. Needless to say, it was Dipti's. On the night before the ceremony, once our hands had been hennaed, someone suggested a stroll through our old haunts. We agreed, and on that cool December night, we found ourselves back on the main street of our childhood, flanked on either side by the bakery and the ice-cream shop. Somehow, we all knew our destination was the bakery. None of us even glanced in the direction of the ice-cream shop.

Its storefront hadn't changed much over the years. The chalkboard still listed the twenty or so main items. The glass display case stocked loaves of familiar breads and pastries whose taste we could recall in our sleep. The man who owned the bakery when we were young came out from behind the counter. He looked small, as if he had shrunk a foot or two. He blinked rapidly, his salt-and-pepper eyebrows raised in surprise. Perhaps we had frightened him by entering his store like a sugar-hungry mob, our faces hidden by our hooded sweatshirts, our bodies sheathed in dark jeans, our hands inexplicably prettied by henna. He peered at our faces. When we told him our names and pointed to the street where we once lived, he broke into a chuckle and apologized for not recognizing anyone.

'Fading memory,' he said, tapping his forehead. 'These days, I only remember the essentials.'

We pointed to the tray of apple strudels displayed in the glass case and ordered four to share. The square pastries were smaller than we remembered. Did they always fit this easily into our palms? We didn't have the patience to wait for an answer. So, we took our first bites, and as our mouths flooded with the taste of cinnamon, raisins and apples, we remembered Miss Josephine and thanked that old, unsmiling woman for the sweet, sweet taste of our childhood.

SHAAJI AND
SATNAM

That Sunday dawned pink and purple, the promise of another lovely, early winter day. Wild chrysanthemums, planted long ago, by unknown hands, nodded along the stretch of green that skirted their village, an unremarkable speck in north-west India. The milkman's cycle trundled down the street, its shrill bell waking up the dogs. The puppies jumped and yipped, but the older ones only yawned with disinterest. They were used to the milkman's daily intrusions.

When the doorbell rang, Shaaji muttered, 'Yes, yes. I am coming, I am coming.' Next to her, her mother snored loudly, a spot of drool drying on her chin. There were deep lines of disapproval etched on her forehead. Shaaji had seen these lines ever since she could remember. For a second, she considered wiping her mother's chin. But then she didn't. Only in sleep could her mother be this loud and free, this uncaring of other people's opinion. Why ruin it?

The bell rang again, this time a long and impatient peal. 'Yes, yes,' Shaaji groaned. 'I'll be right there.' She wrapped a shawl around her shoulders and searched for her slippers on the cold, concrete floor. They lay on top of each other, the toes and heels jutting out at odd angles, the worn leather piled up like corpses.

The baby was fussing in the next room. If the bell rang one more time, he would wake up the entire house. Shaaji hurried downstairs, tiptoeing automatically as she passed her father's room. No, not because he was a light sleeper, but because good girls, girls from families like theirs, walked soundlessly. 'You should never know a girl is in the room,' her father was fond of saying. 'No girl should ever draw attention to herself.'

When she opened the door, the milkman merely gave Shaaji a nod and poured two litres of milk from his metal jug into Shaaji's stainless-steel pot, his slim but well-muscled arms stretching against the slight fabric of his kurta. He was a busy man in the mornings, with no time for idle banter or cosmetic attention. He wore a uniform of sorts every day—a grey kurta-pyjama, and a red-and-white cotton towel to cover his head. Breathable garments all, they were easy to buy, maintain and replicate a thousand times over.

Shaaji shut the door and brought the pot into the kitchen. She could hear voices from upstairs, her oldest brother and his wife, and their still-fussing baby. It wouldn't be long before everyone would troop downstairs in search of their first of many cups of strong, milky tea. She didn't want a mutiny on her hands.

She pulled out five cups and lined them neatly next to the stove. She counted again—one, two, three, four, five— just to be sure and then ran to the downstairs bathroom to change into one of her mother's saris. Ordinarily, she didn't like wearing saris, but today was different. Today, it was her armour, though onlookers might say its broad, peach flowers didn't automatically suggest war. She smiled as she remembered that Satnam liked her in saris. He would lick a finger and dart it like a bolt of lightning across her navel. That one dot of wet skin would make her go weak in the knees, its memory alone enough of a burn to keep her awake at night.

When she re-entered the drawing room with the tea tray, they were all there, circled like a small army. Her younger brother was scratching his chin and staring out of the window, hoping to catch a glimpse of the young widow across the street. Her older brother was reading the sports section of the newspaper, while his wife bounced their son on her knee, trying to calm him down. Shaaji wondered how it would feel once the baby stopped crying. Probably nothing. Their village was noisy enough to absorb every silence.

Only her mother looked up as Shaaji began handing out the tea. She ran her eyes over her daughter's choice of sari and opened her mouth, as if to say something. But her husband spoke up. 'Good,' he murmured, his one word enough for the two of them.

Shaaji dropped her head and absorbed her father's compliment. 'Good' and 'decent'—the only two words he considered appropriate if he ever felt the need to praise his daughter. Even now, in spite of knowing better, it was this that Shaaji craved the most.

She watched them sip their teas. No one asked her about her morning or why she wasn't drinking any. One by one, they fell asleep, right there in their respective spots, threads of saliva hinging their mouths to their chins, their faces still turned towards their objects of attention, whether it was the nubile widow or the day's cricket update. Her father's glasses slid off from his nose, cracking as they hit the concrete floor. The shards cascaded like silver rain. Thankfully, he would never need to use them again.

Shaaji caught the baby just as her sister-in-law's grip loosened. Cooing, she took her nephew to the kitchen and fed him two spoons of the milk. As expected, he fell asleep faster than the adults. Gently, she placed him on the floor and studied the room. Sure, her family members were all over the place, but besides that, was everything else in its right place? Was everything neat and tidy? She straightened a cushion that had fallen off and swept up the glass shards with a broom. Satnam mustn't doubt her housekeeping skills.

The bell rang and Shaaji carefully skirted around her sleeping nephew to open the door. Once again, it was the milkman. Except that it wasn't. It was Satnam dressed as the milkman. He had done an excellent job imitating the loose folds of the red-and-white turban. The grey kurta-pyjama was identical, as was the milk jug, both bought last month at the city fair.

Though she couldn't see his eyes clearly—the shadow of the turban bisected his face in half—Shaaji felt the same longing she had the first time she had seen him at the bus stop. They were both sixteen, on their way to school, when he had asked her name. It still seemed like yesterday but in reality, it had already been two years. Two years of stolen kisses and Satnam's rough-farmhand fingers scorching her thighs, stomach and breasts with his touch; of her mother finding out and nearly ripping her hair from its roots and then fasting to rid her of this evil; of her brothers' threats to wipe out Satnam's entire family; of her father pulling her out of school; of her sister-in-law slapping her so hard that she still had trouble hearing from her left ear. But Shaaji had forgiven her mother and sister-in-law. It wasn't entirely their fault. It is an unwritten rule after all—old victims must forever be in search of new ones to take their place. The only bright spots in these two years were the secret meetings with Satnam and his letters that her best friend smuggled in for Shaaji inside her bra.

Satnam brushed past Shaaji and entered the room. He smelled like he always did, of cigarettes and deodorant, and the pit of Shaaji's stomach tingled with longing. It had been her idea. She hoped the milkman would understand that framing him wasn't personal. It was because he and Satnam were of similar height and build. In another life, where caste and religion would be mere words, the two could have been brothers. This step was to ensure that if anyone, say the widow, happened to be watching from the streets, they would see the milkman brushing past Shaaji's mother.

The choice of sari was a fine touch. The neighbours must have lost count of how often Shaaji's mother dressed in that peach print. They would think the milkman was there to drop off an extra litre or two, after all there was a baby in the house, or to pick up his monthly wage.

Later, a devastated Shaaji would tell the police that the milkman had always had a thing for her. That's why he had first drugged the milk, then sawed off the necks of her family members—not the baby, the baby he had strangled—and then forced himself on her. It was only the chance arrival of Satnam that had scared him away.

Shaaji watched as Satnam unscrewed the lid of the milk jug. He was biting the inside of his lower lip, a habit she found endearing. Slowly, as if he was handling a baby, he pulled out yet another recent purchase. An axe. He had sharpened it the night before. Humming to herself, Shaaji traced her little finger against a peach flower. Soon the white background would be stained red. Shaaji began humming a Hindi song, a favourite of both of them—*dil hain ki manta nahin* (the heart knows no reason). Satnam looked up, smiling. So what if she drew attention to herself once in a while? She had thought of everything else, hadn't she? She was a good girl after all, like her father had always wanted.

IF ONLY

SOMEWHERE

Shaaji and Satnam, Ten Years Later

It wasn't meant to go this far. When the boy strode into the store that afternoon, Shaaji couldn't help but wonder how handsome he would be if he didn't have such a horrible limp. For every step he took with his left foot, his right foot followed a second later, like an afterthought, like the kid nobody wanted to sit next to in class. With his thick hair, square face and full lips, he reminded her of Aamir Khan in *Qayamat Se Qayamat Tak* (QSQT). He should be on the cover of a glossy magazine, Shaaji thought, or staring down at us lesser mortals from sky-high, expensive hoardings. She had watched *QSQT* when she was ten, although the film had been out for at least a few years by then. She had been at a neighbour's home, playing with their baby, when the mother had switched on the small black-and-white TV and arranged herself in front of it.

There it was—an entire, full-length Hindi film that Shaaji could just sit and watch. No mother wringing her hands helplessly in the background, torn between the desire for a

111

little time for herself and duty towards the seven people in the house. No father yanking off the cord, screaming and shouting that the TV was only for news. No older brothers echoing the words of their father and yet staring every night into the gleaming blue light of their shared desktop, shooing her away if she so much as paused at their doorway.

Of course, she had had to beg the neighbour lady. But that hadn't been a problem. In villages like theirs, women knew how to keep little girls' secrets. Plus, Shaaji had always excelled at minding babies.

The boy with the limp pointed to a pack of Charminar. Shaaji plucked it off the shelf and placed it on the counter. Yes, he was a young Aamir all right. The dip in the chin, the hint of a mischievous smile and the lanky frame.

Unexpectedly, he broke into a smile. 'Remember me?' he asked. One of his eyebrows shot up.

Shaaji blinked. A memory bloomed, faint and cloudy at first, then gradually taut around the edges until it pulled tight. 'Of course!' she squealed, smacking her head, forgetting it was still tender. Satnam's hands were like hammers.

'How long has it been?' she asked loudly, hoping it would distract him from her wince and her swiftly watering eyes. 'Five years? Six years? Where have you been this entire time?' She saw him now as he had been once—twelve or thirteen years old, sucking on hard-boiled mango candies, begging for a little more of the spicy chanachur she made at home and sold at the store in small glass jars.

'Delhi,' the boy replied, a touch of pride in his voice.

'Oooh, Delhi! You're a big-city, fancy man now? That's why these bad habits,' Shaaji pointedly looked at the Charminar.

'This is nothing!' the boy laughed. 'You don't know what Delhi boys my age do for fun. If I don't try now, when will I? When I am your age?'

'Achcha?' Shaaji laughed. 'One tight slap you will get from me.'

'I am so happy you remember me! I have run into three people so far, all of whom have looked right through me. I've had to remind them. Loudly.'

'Forget them!' Shaaji said dismissively, waving a hand. 'Tell me, do you still love spicy chanachur?'

'No. Remember, I am a big-city, fancy man now?'

They both laughed at that. This boy, now a man, she had got to know when she and Satnam had first moved into this town, before Babu was born, before they bought this store. How sweet and unexpected was this moment! How precious this laughter. It dissolved Shaaji's reality like the first drop of rain on scorching asphalt. This was so much more than a conversation in this godforsaken town, two thousand kilometres away from the other godforsaken town where she had been born and raised, and whose clutches she and Satnam had escaped.

This moment was perfect, like the first bite of a tart lemon pickle.

~

Later, Shaaji would relive the moment again and again. If she could yank back time, crumple it between her hands like paper and toss it away, this would be the moment she would choose.

She and the boy shouldn't have laughed.

He shouldn't have come into the store.

She shouldn't have recognized him.

He shouldn't have raised a jaunty eyebrow.

She shouldn't have liked his face nor called him 'Young Aamir' in her mind.

So many shouldn'ts.

But the moment did occur. How was she to know that they weren't alone? That Satnam had returned from the mandi and was outside? Listening. Waiting.

As soon as the boy with the limp left, Satnam entered the store. He was biting the inside of his lower lip, a sure sign of anger or nervousness, or both. This habit hadn't changed, although in these last ten years there had been other changes. He had spread in the middle. Now, he wore pants two sizes bigger than what he used to, and his temples had more grey hair than black.

A familiar curdling sensation bubbled inside Shaaji's stomach. She ran her tongue over her teeth, as if to clear the foul taste. Her head throbbed from its last painful memory. She braced herself. For now, there would only be words. They were in public after all, in this store of theirs that he'd set up right in the middle of the market. She squared her shoulders and stood straight. The only way she could help herself was by looking less guilty. She answered Satnam's questions as they fell on her. She remembered how her two brothers used to lob pebbles at stray dogs in the neighbourhood. They would laugh at her protests. 'This is for fun,' they would say.

Yes, she knew she was no longer a young girl.

No, she wasn't flirting.

Yes, she knew she was Babu's mother.

Yes, she knew she was Satnam's wife.

No, she didn't want Babu to think his mother was a whore.

No, she didn't want the village to think Satnam's wife was a whore.

Yes, she cared for Babu deeply.

Yes, boys his age would be devastated if they learned their mother was a whore.

Shaaji stared at her feet, at the peeling fuchsia paint on her toenails, and waited for the words to stop. Satnam stood by the wall where they hung the calendars and pictures. He knocked on it lightly, rhythmically, his long, slim fingers so unlike what they turned into in the privacy of their home. 'I am asking you for the last time . . . What did the *chamar* want?"

'Bread,' Shaaji said without thinking. She cursed herself immediately. *Why did she say bread? Why not tell the truth? Why not just say cigarettes?*

'Bread?' Satnam's eyes narrowed. 'Are you sure?'

Shaaji nodded furiously. Was it too late to change her answer? Could she say she had made a mistake? She had misheard his question? She kept her head lowered, a convict about to be punished. Her fuchsia toenails looked hideous. Her feet looked gnarly. She knew he didn't believe her.

'I could have sworn I saw him leave with a pack of cigarettes. No?'

'No.' Shaaji strained her ears for the sound of approaching customers. She heard the honks of the mid-afternoon buses, the radio trilling from the tyre shop next door. Babu would be home in an hour. She had to wrap this up before then. She tried again. 'Maybe he bought the cigarettes before he came in? Yes, I am sure he had them on him when he came in.'

A shadow fell across the floor. It was Deodhar, the owner of the tyre shop. As always, his grocery list was scribbled on his right palm. Shaaji spurred into action. She filled up Deodhar's bags with eggs, rice, lentils and butter. Satnam clapped Deodhar on the arm. They made small talk as if they were brothers. Shaaji tossed in a handful of mango candies for the kids.

'You shouldn't. You always spoil them,' Deodhar said, a tone of reproach in his voice that he didn't mean. He liked getting free things. He liked that his sons had turned out exactly like him.

The interrogation resumed as soon as Deodhar left. Satnam gripped Shaaji's left wrist. It was always the left wrist. 'I am asking you for the final time,' he said, his words scraping through his gritted teeth. 'Why did the chamar have his phone out? What was he showing to you? Were you exchanging numbers?'

'No! Please. He is only a kid. I beg you. I didn't notice his phone.'

'Why were you two smiling so much?'

'Were we? I don't know. I don't know, believe me. He said I was the only one who recognized him. Maybe that's why.' She felt Satnam's grip tighten. Her body shook like she was nothing more than a bird. Neither of her long-sleeved blouses—that came all the way down to her wrists—were clean. She would have to wash one as soon as she was home. As soon as she had laid out Babu's food, that is. Hopefully, he would leave her alone for a few minutes and not follow her around the house with yet another barrage of questions. *Where do clouds come from, Ma? Who made the sun? Today, in school we learned about the sun. Do birds talk to each other?*

Sometimes, Shaaji marvelled at her son, at his curiosity for the world, his eagerness to swallow it whole as if it were a magic fruit. She wanted to ask him, 'Where do your questions come from, son? When I was your age, all I wanted to do was watch movies. How do you see the world so differently?' But she never asked. The only thing she knew for sure was that Babu was his father's son. He was a little man full of wonder.

Satnam finally let go of her wrist. 'Believe you?' he spat. His voice shook. So much time had passed, so many moments had come and gone, but still, he couldn't contain the tremble in those words.

Shaaji locked eyes with her husband. For a fleeting second his armour dropped, and she saw the hurt. She thought of the man he had been, the one she had loved, and how she had believed he was saving her from her father, and from a future where she would end up just like her mother, married and invisible.

'Believe you,' Satnam repeated, as if he was trying.

~

That night, Satnam didn't come to bed. Shaaji hoped he was balancing books or drinking with Deodhar. Sometimes, the men forgot they were husbands and fathers and went prowling at night in search of toys and playthings that weren't theirs, but that they still wanted. Close to dawn, Shaaji heard the creak of the main door. In the adjoining room, Babu stirred and mumbled something in his asleep.

She heard Satnam climbing the stairs, one drunken stumble after another. Once upon a time, the mere hint of him was enough to ignite every inch of her skin. After they got married, they spent countless nights like that, entwined, his beautiful fingers tracing circles on her body. *Hush, Shaaji,* he would admonish. *Don't giggle so much. Hold still. I am writing a secret message.* In those moments, when their need for each other outweighed everything, she almost forgave the monster she was and the monster she had married.

Which is why when Ramesh entered her life, Shaaji wasn't prepared for it. He was their neighbour in the first city they moved to after they eloped, the one they lived in before they came here. Ramesh was a schoolteacher unlike any she had ever known. The ones from her childhood smelled of boredom, bad breath, classrooms that were too small, and necks and armpits that needed washing. They taught from books that were exactly like them, dull and awful, devoid of curiosity and imagination.

Ramesh had knocked on her door because he had run out of salt. 'For my dal,' he had said, holding up a small, stainless-steel bowl. When she had filled it up and brought it to him, he had asked her the most bizarre question. 'Did you know that the Romans believed that Neptune, their god of water and sea, was married to the goddess of salt?'

Shaaji hadn't known how to react. So, she hadn't. But for hours afterwards, Ramesh's question had spun in her mind. She didn't know the Romans or why they needed or wanted a goddess of salt. But why not? If they could have Annapurna, the goddess of grain, why couldn't others worship salt? What an odd fact, and yet, this strange man had shared it with such great and obvious delight in his voice. As if he was giving her a gift. If only it had stopped there. At this one gift.

But it didn't. It was Ramesh who taught Shaaji that in a place called Strasbourg in Europe, in 1518, several people died from something called the dancing plague. That human heartbeats change to the beat of the music one is listening to. That apparently, Sultan Ibrahim I had two hundred and eighty of his concubines drowned because one of them had been unfaithful to him. That in flamingos, both mothers and fathers produce milk and feed their babies, and that the birds come in colours as vibrant as orange and pink. And that when you kiss, you feel the things you do, in your mouth, stomach and all the way down to your toes because of the crazy chemical cocktail in your brain. Shaaji didn't understand how any one person could know so much, but she understood this—there was no one like Ramesh, and second, why had no one ever told her that she loved learning.

Shaaji felt Satnam's hands fumbling for her in the dark. She squeezed her eyes and he climbed over her, his breath a cocktail of sweat, dirt, booze and oily food. She didn't protest when his hands cinched her waist, when his drunken fingers tugged at the string of her petticoat, when in this situation too, it was her left wrist that he gripped the hardest.

~

The next time Shaaji saw the boy with the limp, he was the headline and main news story in their local newspaper. He no longer looked like he could star in *QSQT*. He had been found in the fields, two days too late, his good leg now impossible to tell from his bad one.

The local police had launched a routine investigation. Nothing urgent or highbrow. They marched from one home to another, asking the same half-hearted questions over and over again, interviewing the men in their front yards and the women shimmering in the shadows within. Caste wars were as regular here as night and day, so Brahmin cops interrogated Brahmins, the Gurjars tackled their own, and so on.

By the time they arrived at the store to interview Shaaji, the policemen's faces were slick with sweat, the collars of their shirts drenched and pasted to their backs. She poured them tall glasses of cold water. They drank furiously, then splashed it on their faces and the backs of their necks, and asked for refills.

The officer-in-charge pulled out a dirty handkerchief and wiped his brow. 'Did you know the boy?'

'I knew he was from the village,' Shaaji said. She wondered if he would ask why she was wearing a long, thick blouse in the middle of summer.

'Did you know he was visiting from Delhi?'

'Yes, he stopped by on his first day. He came to buy cigarettes.' With her right thumb, Shaaji rubbed her left wrist, where the latest bruise was as dark and purple as a plum.

'Cigarettes, huh? Not beedi?' The officer shook his head as if the boy's choice of addiction explained everything. He turned to his constables. 'What do I always say? One should never overreach?'

'Yes, cigarettes,' Shaaji repeated. She rubbed her left wrist again. Would he notice if she pulled back the fabric?

'Did you notice anything suspicious?'

'No. He seemed happy to be home.'

'Did you know him well?'

'Not at all. I hadn't seen him in years.'

'Hmm . . . one last question . . .' the officer paused, his voice trailing, his eyes finally caught on her left wrist. 'Do you know if he had any enemies?' His eyes narrowed, as if trying to make sense of the marks on Shaaji's wrist.

She felt the bruise thrum. It was aware of the attention, and given the chance, it would bloom, bear fruit and fly. Shaaji wondered how it would be if the colour spread, if it seeped through her skin. If it turned her into a purple flamingo. Inside her throat, a scream built up like a dust storm. She imagined Babu boarding his school bus, running along their neighbour's wheat field, rummaging through her carefully stocked larders of rice and lentils in search of the chocolates she playfully hid from him. She imagined the questions he would ask if either of his parents went away. She thought of the chickens pecking in her backyard, their heads nodding like old women and the goats ambling along the fence. One day, Babu would inherit it all, their home, this shop, their backyard with its tiny population of two-legged and four-legged beasts. She thought of flamingos, of how they make excellent parents and how she had never seen one except in a large book of birds, the pages flapping under the breeze of a noisy ceiling fan, the same fan from which Ramesh was found hanging, two days after Satnam learned of his existence.

Shaaji pulled down the sleeve of her blouse. She clasped her hands together and the bruise disappeared from the policemen's gaze. For some crimes, like secretly watching an Aamir Khan movie, there is forgiveness. For others, like plotting and abetting the murder of one's entire family, there is heart-crushing punishment and a lifetime of guilt. Babu needed both his parents.

Shaaji shook her head. 'Sorry, I don't know anything else.'

The officer didn't move a muscle.

Shaaji adjusted her face until it broke into a pleading smile. 'Sorry, sir. It's my son. He must be on his way home from school now. He will be hungry and tired. I have to tend to him. Boys this age can be so demanding.'

THE
WAITRESS

Twice already, the blonde waitress with cranberry lips has paused by her table and asked, 'Can I interest you in something?' Both times, Sia has politely shaken her head and thought the same thing: 'Button up your shirt, sweetheart. Any more cleavage and your employer will have to install a pole.'

The third time, though, Sia relents. 'A glass of the house red, please,' she says, her eyes flitting to the door.

The waitress nods and returns to the bar, the outline of her panties clearly visible through her tight black dress. Sia makes a disapproving noise, but it is lost in the loud music. She rubs her arms. Why is Raja late for his own birthday celebration? How can he keep her waiting when he knows how much she hates The Castle and its godawful smell of stale beer, fried food and unwashed jeans? She's here only because it's *his* birthday. She's here because *he* thinks The Castle is a hoot, 'a classic bar with history'. If it was up to her, she would never step inside these yellow walls nor sit at these chipped-tile, maize-yellow Formica tables, the colours neither warm nor welcoming.

Minute by minute, The Castle fills up with its usual crowd—college students, recent alums who seem unsure of what they are still doing here, and a few professors and townsfolk, desperately and helplessly trying to hold on to their youth. Unlike Sia, the regulars don't care about how The Castle looks or how poorly it has aged. They're here for the shots, the karaoke machine, the notoriously easy hook-ups, and the two tricks the two bartenders know between themselves—the Flourish, where they whorl the napkin right before placing the drink upon it, and the self-explanatory Multipour.

The tricks had caught Sia's eye the first time, and she had tipped generously. But by her next visit, it had become clear that that's all they knew. No, sir, thank you very much! She was a broke grad student, and she was not going to throw her hard-earned teaching assistantship-money on these clowns.

'Thanks,' Sia says stiffly, as the waitress places a glass of red wine before her. She takes a sip and remembers her first time at The Castle. That, too, had been for a birthday, her room-mate Elly's. It had been barely a month since her arrival in America. Her brain felt divided, as if half of it was back home in Jaipur. Everything was new and strange here, starting with her dorm room and room-mates, who couldn't have been more different from one another. While Lisa preferred staying home and playing with her cats, Elly was the queen of side hustles, switching back and forth between her jobs as a tattoo artist, a nude model for the local art school and as a part-time barista.

Then there were Sia's professors, who required her to participate in every group discussion, seminar and lecture. But the worst was having to do her own laundry in the very publicly located laundromat, while jostling others for available machines, counting exact change and that too only in quarters, and having to see, smell and brush past other people's soiled clothes. One time, she ran out of quarters, and for the following week, had to wash her underwear in the bathroom sink. Another time, the machine swallowed her clothes and wouldn't open. Not to mention the countless times she added too much or too little soap, or forgot to grab the pack of dryer sheets.

Sia sips, and then sips again. The wine warms her throat and she hears her mother's voice, shrill and distinct. *Shameless. Hussy.* Despite the continents and oceans between them, the disdain and disappointment are as clear as if she was right here, at this table. '*This*,' Sia thinks fiercely as tears sting her eyes. She scratches a corner of the table. 'This is far better than *that* any day.' She will never return to Jaipur, she promises herself again. She will never return to the claustrophobia of her joint family nor go anywhere within a kilometre of the convent school where she suffered for twelve stifling years. Never again will she set foot in that barbaric neighbourhood in which she grew up, where even a chance conversation with a boy could taint your reputation for weeks.

For really, there is nothing quite like having choices, is there? A hundred rounds to the laundromat are preferable to Papa's permanent scowl, his lips stretched into a thin line of displeasure over yet another setback in their garment business. Had he ever said a kind word to Sia? Or to anyone for that matter? Or did he truly believe that the grunts he deigned to grant to the world were enough communication?

Perhaps it was to compensate for his silences that Ma talked so much, her words tripping over one another, like a mountain river tumbling over rocks. So eager she was to please everyone, so nervous of what they might say to dismiss her, her husband, or her child-rearing skills.

If Papa had had choices, would he have become an artist? He doodled any time he sat by himself. On newspapers, brown paper bags, receipts, ledgers—the material didn't matter. He covered them up with fish, monkeys, people, parrots and trees. He *had* to draw. His fingers couldn't still themselves.

And Ma? Had she known the concept of choice, she would have probably married into a family that didn't routinely remind her that she was still the daughter-in-law who had brought in the least amount of dowry, a family that would have let her eat and breathe in peace, drink a glass of red wine if she wanted to.

The thought of her mother's flabby fingers circling the thin stem of a wine glass makes Sia giggle. She looks for Raja again. Last night, when he had yanked her to him, she had responded enthusiastically. She had grabbed him by his collar and sucked on his neck.

'Whoa, easy there,' Raja had cried.

Sia licks her lips, as if she can still taste his skin and cologne. *This* is why she is here, at The Castle. To grab life by its collar and suck in its choices. To celebrate Raja's birthday, and then in a few weeks, their one-year anniversary, then two, three, and so on. She wasn't supposed to think so far ahead but what if, and here Sia scrunches her eyes and thinks intently, what if she suggests moving in together? Too soon? What would Raja say? And what would her parents say? Would Papa vanish in a cloud of rage? And Ma? Would she throw a fit, wait to see everyone else's reaction, then react some more.

A finger tickles the back of her neck. Sia jumps from her chair and hugs Raja. 'You're here,' she beams. 'Happy birthday, sweetheart! I didn't see you come in.'

Raja says, 'You looked lost in thought.' He hooks his fingers into the waistband of her jeans and pulls her towards himself.

Sia blushes. She looks around, but there is no need. Not one person at The Castle has stirred in their direction. No one's curious. No one cares. She allows herself to imagine how such a moment would have played out at Chandan Sweets, the food joint closest to her home. How everyone, from the waiters to the owner to the customers would have reacted. She breathes in as Raja's fingers lift her shirt, oh so slightly, and stroke her skin. How could anyone make old blue jeans and a frayed white shirt look this effortless?

Raja winks and leans in for a kiss. Sia knows she isn't so bad herself. She is tall for an Indian woman, and Raja tells her every day that she is Miss Tits Extraordinaire. She knows her hair and eyes are her other good features. Gosh, their children will be good-looking, won't they?

Stop it, you idiot, she hisses. Most importantly, Raja and her kids will grow up knowing they can be whoever they want. They can be a baker like their dad, or a physicist like their mother. Traditional gender roles be damned! They will be loved and not scolded for sneaking a puff of an uncle's cigarette (*have you no shame, Sia*), for not bringing home a stellar report card (*all you do is dream about boys, Sia*), for not excelling at music class (*must you always be such a poor role model, Sia; don't you know the younger kids are watching you, Sia*).

Raja lets go of her and sits down. He snaps his fingers. 'Hello, Lady S? Are you there?'

Sia sighs happily. 'I love it when you call me that.' And then she adds, 'You know, if I put things in perspective and remember the garbage I had to put up with from my family, this bar is nothing short of a five-star restaurant, and my tiny apartment with Lisa and Elly a luxurious penthouse.'

'That bad, huh?' Raja asks.

'You have no idea,' Sia says, reaching across the table for Raja's hands. 'Anyway, forget about me. Today's all about you. Tell me how we should celebrate you.' Sia drops her voice conspiratorially. If you want, I can take a stab at the karaoke. Sing you a song? Embarrass you, me and all my ancestors? No? Then how about I beg the bartender to name a drink after you. Or declare our old slutty waitress the Queen of the Universe.'

Raja laughs. He scans the bar. 'I don't care if she is old or slutty. I just want a drink.'

Sia gestures with her eyes. 'The one with boobs up to her ears.'

Raja waves to attract the waitress's attention. When she arrives, he chats about the weather and puts in his order for a beer.

Sia draws her knees together under the table. On top of being this irresistible, Raja is also a nice guy. 'Happy birthday, my love,' Sia whispers. She stares at the cheap black dress of their waitress, at her retreating panty line, and thinks *slut, slut, slut*. She promises to find them a new hang-out spot. Raja deserves better, something chic and sophisticated, like the future she is planning for them.

~

Sydney sucks on the insides of her cheeks until a tight ball of spit gathers at the tip of her tongue. She pokes her head out from behind the kitchen curtain as if to check on orders but swiftly spits into the two cocktails the bartender has put on her tray. No one sees her. The bartender's back stays turned towards her. She gives the drinks a quick stir with their too-bright, too-happy, too-pointless umbrellas and walks purposefully to her customers, glancing en route at the large mirror by the bar to check her reflection.

When did she first spit into a drink? Sydney can't remember. Was it on a dare perhaps? Maybe. She remembers making a shit ton in tips that night, and the subsequent birthing of a superstition.

Sydney drops off the drinks and circles back to the mirror. Her cranberry lipstick is still fresh, her boobs proud and perky. But they won't help tonight. Tuesdays are the worst for tips, and she has several payments due this week—rent, car insurance, health insurance, groceries, electricity, water and heat. On top of that, Davey needs a new winter coat. He has outgrown the one from last year. Then there are new snow boots and a new backpack. And these are just the basics. It's mid-November already, and she has no idea how to get even one of the items Davey has requested for Christmas.

It crushes Sydney to think of her son when she is stuck at work. Of course she is biased, but Davey is a great kid. He is quiet and studious, he doesn't ask for much, or for anything at all, except during Christmas. Who does he take after? Sydney wonders for the billionth time. Not her—she has never been quiet or studious. Most definitely not after his dad. The last time she saw that guy, Davey was three months old.

He is seven now. Stuck at their neighbour's home while she is at work. At least he is warm and safe, and most days, he and June get along well. Table 7 clears and Sydney rushes to wipe it down. There's a measly three-dollar tip stuck under the coaster, but she doesn't mind. She likes the customer. He's a regular, and he has sad eyes, but he always says hello to her in the nicest way possible.

Sydney gives the area under the table a quick sweep. June is such an old-fashioned name for a six-year-old girl. Really, what had Molly been thinking? But that's probably the only thing common between her and Molly. They are both single moms who should have thought harder about some of their choices.

She assumes her usual spot by the bar and cracks her knuckles. She stares at the entrance, willing the doors to swing open. It's unfair that Davey knows Molly's kitchen better than he knows their own. He has learned valuable lessons there—how to clear a table, fix himself a bowl of cereal, water the plant by the sink without spilling water, how to rinse a plate.

Sydney bites her lip. She hasn't taught Davey a thing. Where is the time? She works nights while he stays at Molly's, and when she sleeps during the day, he is away at school.

To be fair, Molly's kitchen isn't a terrible place to get to know. It's clean, and Molly's salary as a kindergarten teacher allows her to buy real food. Sure, it's not that organic shit, but it's definitely not anything trashy out of a box. Maybe in the long run all this will work out okay for Davey. Maybe, despite everything, he will become someone fancy. Like a chef. Chefs earned well, didn't they? They travelled the world; they did TV shows; they wrote fat books with glossy pictures; they owned restaurants and gyms, and God knows what else. Even the whale-sized, wheezing chef here earned five times what she took home every month.

Sydney closes her eyes and leans against the wall. Surely their lives will improve by the time Davey's a teenager. Six years isn't that far. She would have love in her life by then, won't she? Teenage Davey would need more things—better shoes; an actual room of his own; maybe clothes that aren't always from thrift stores; haircuts by someone with a licence instead of by his mom over the bathroom sink; maybe he would have a guitar too, and a dad, or a dad-like figure. Someone who would keep him in line and make sure he didn't end up as yet another statistic in this Podunk town.

There were too many problems here. Too many distractions. Temptations and choices waiting to trip you up. One time, a customer, a brainy, professor-type at that, had told her about 'decision fatigue'. You ended up shooting yourself in the foot when you had too many choices and decisions to make.

At least for now, Davey was okay. He was still her little man. Late last night, she had picked up his sleeping form from Molly's couch. She had tucked him into his own bed and he had sleepily said, 'I love you, Mom.' Her throat had clenched and she had fought hard to keep the tears at bay. 'I love you more, pumpkin,' she had said, kissing his cheek before collapsing on the heap of washed and unwashed clothes that constituted her bed.

Sydney's eyes sweep over the three occupied tables, before they train on the entrance again, willing crowds to burst through the doors. 'Come on, you drunkards,' she urges, 'My baby and I need your money.' An unexpected gust of wind blows in from somewhere, but it does not bring with it any new customers.

Her gaze pulls back to the table at the end, to the Indian woman—girl, really—and her boyfriend. The girl's gorgeous to look at. Full boobs, beautiful skin, delicate features. She isn't a regular here, and she has knocked back her wine too quickly. Either she is nervous or keen to appear sophisticated to her boyfriend.

Sydney hasn't liked the way the girl has looked at her—coolly, as if appraising and dismissing her. She has known women and girls like this all her life. They have called her a bimbo, floozy and much worse.

An acrid taste fills the inside of Sydney's mouth. She wants to march up to the girl, grab her by the shoulders and smack her hard across the face. Who the hell does she think she is? If she is so much better than everyone else, why is she here? Why not go to the snooty new bar downtown, the one with the red brick walls and fairy lights, and the overpriced appetizer plates called 'littles'?

Sydney pulls out her phone. There are two unread texts. The first is from her bank warning her about the overdrawn state of her account. The second is from Erik asking, 'Any bites tonight?' She deletes both the messages and puts her phone away. No, she won't do it. It had been great to go home with the thick roll of cash, and even though she had spent the money quickly, it was as if a rock had been placed on her chest every time she tried to eat or drink or do anything else. For weeks, she had slept poorly, imagining the girl, the men,

Erik's truck and his soft fingers—that entire whirlpool of money, motels and transactions.

But if she did it, it *would* make her life so simple. Just one text to Erik. That is all. When she had begged to leave after she got pregnant with Davey, Erik had agreed, but on one condition. Sydney's silence and continued cooperation. 'There is nothing to prove anyway, Syd,' he had murmured, kissing her neck as if they were still lovers. 'You were already a whore, baby. I didn't turn you into one.'

Even now, so many years later, his words wounded like the serrated edge of a knife. Of course it was Erik's doing. How could she have known any better? She was fourteen. Her father was dead, her mother barely able to function.

And Erik?

He was right there, this older man with impeccable looks and manners, with eyes and smiles full of attention, an arsenal of sweet words and the willingness to pick her up and take her to places, to impromptu lunches and dinners, friends' parties, weekend trips to Spokane, and eventually, to and from motels and customers. She had tried to break away so many times, and each time she had failed, until Davey had come along, and then she had begged, promising Erik she wouldn't go anywhere, that she would be right here, under his nose, that she would work for him and he would always know where to find her.

Sydney shifts on her feet. Maybe next month she will try to look for a pair of cheap shoes online. She inhales deeply, her eyes on the couple in the corner. Sydney watches the two of them. The boyfriend wants to stay, but the girl keeps trying to leave. They could leave if they wanted to. For now, all Erik will need is a picture of her and her car. He will do the rest. In a small town like theirs, and especially with his range of contacts, tracking anyone takes minutes.

He invested time in what he called 'research'. Studying the girl's habits, comings and goings, likes and dislikes, loves and hatreds, all her social media handles. He had told her once, 'This part can't be rushed, Syd. Each girl must be seasoned differently. What works on a thirteen-year-old won't on a twenty-one-year-old.'

Once, many years ago, Sydney had tried telling Molly everything. But sweet Molly, a newly appointed kindergarten teacher, had only rolled her eyes. 'Stop it, will you? Trafficking? In our little town where everyone knows everyone? Please, Syd, this is still America, not some shithole country with no law and order.'

~

'Wow, look at those wrinkles,' Sia thinks as the overhead lamp highlights the waitress' face and settles on the brackets around her eyes and mouth. 'White women age so quickly. Should I tell her she isn't sixteen any more? The cleavage show isn't fooling anyone?' Sia pinches her lips together so as to not burst out laughing. She hooks her purse over her shoulder. She urges Raja to his feet, 'Come, darling, let's go. Let's continue celebrating your birthday.'

~

It is late afternoon when Sydney stumbles into her bathroom. She splashes water over her face, slowly at first and then rapidly, in large fistfuls. She wants to wake up but also drown, as memories of the previous night come rushing in like a rockslide.

If only that stupid Indian girl had let her say what she says to every customer every night. *Thank you, guys, for coming in! You have a good one.* But she hadn't. She hadn't heard a word of what Sydney had to say. She hadn't looked her in the eyes even once. Instead, she had hummed at her boyfriend like a bitch in heat. *Let's go, darling. Let's continue celebrating your birthday.*

What a whore. What a goddamn, fucking whore.

Truthfully though, it wasn't the words. It wasn't even the accent, though it was strong. Sydney didn't care whether anyone was foreign or brown or yellow or spoke English or not. Once they were inside The Castle, they were her customers.

It was the girl's tone. When she had said those words to her boyfriend, she had sounded so trusting, so saturated with love that it was stupid. It was how Sydney used to be, before everything unravelled, before she turned fourteen, before she met Erik, when there was someone else, a sweet boy her age, Stephen, and one afternoon after school he had invited her to go to a diner with him. They had spent two hours there, eating burgers and fries, listening to the scratchy speakers announcing every few minutes: *Free, free, free, our 2-for-1 deal until 3, 3, 3!*

Sydney returns to her bedroom, her face wet and puffy. She grabs her phone from the nightstand. The battery is down to less than 10 per cent, but there are no missed calls or voicemails or texts. She tosses it back on the nightstand and waits for it to die.

When her stomach lets out a rumble, Sydney grabs a spoon and a can of tuna from the kitchen. She pries open the lid and dives into the salty fish. She nearly gags, but she doesn't stop. She chews and swallows, then opens the almost-empty fridge and finishes the last of Davey's chocolate milk.

She makes a mental to-do list. She will pay the phone company, the car-insurance people and her landlord. Once Davey returns from school, she will take him shopping. She will buy everything he needs, and then some more just for fun. She will stock up their fridge with chocolate milk, fruits, carrots and salad. Later, mother and son will watch a movie. She will let Davey choose. He will probably pick *Despicable Me* again. Before the movie starts, they will order pizzas. Pepperoni, Davey's favourite, and mushrooms and onions, hers. She will sit with her plate in front of the TV. She will laugh and eat, laugh, laugh, eat, eat, until her insides are stuffed with bread and cheese, until the food reaches her eyes, then her brain, and wipes away every memory of the Indian girl's face.

ANOTHER
LIFE

Kolkata, August 2010

Mrs Desai's eyes sprang open as if escaping a nightmare. Outside her window, the monsoon rain beat down on the concrete and glass and flooded her vegetable garden. For several days now, she had been sleeping poorly. No matter how many times she willed her ears to block every sound except the comforting rut-a-tut-tut-a whirr of the ceiling fan, a good night's rest was proving to be elusive.

The wet-earth aroma of the garden gushed in like a swollen river. As tired as she was of the rain, the smell made Mrs Desai inhale deeply and mutter 'guru . . . guru' under her breath. There it was. That one solitary word uttered twice. Her constant stress-reliever, her anchor in this ever-changing world of insanity. Chanted like a prayer but buried like a secret so that no one heard her, not even her husband of forty years who slept peacefully, his mouth open like a cave on a hillside, seemingly at peace with the universe.

The room was aglow with the faint light of dawn. Mrs Desai sat up and put on her thick glasses. On the wall straight ahead, an impressive array of postcards looked back at her from inside black frames. They exhibited grass that had turned red in fall and turquoise lakes with only the faintest reflection of the moon. There were tall trees with trunks so brown that they looked black, their branches open as if welcoming the world for an embrace, and leaves that glowed like jewels—amber, jasper, red beryl and rubies. Mrs Desai rubbed her hands and feet and murmured the names of these places—lakes as unfamiliar as Redfish, Payette and Coeur d'Alene, forests of huckleberry that reminded her of characters from well-loved books, and mountains called Sawtooth that suggested untold perils. The postcards were from Idaho, where her nephew Dev lived with his American wife, Kathy, and where her brother Arun had spent his last days. Shortly before his death, Arun had sent her these postcards. He had urged her to visit. 'You have to come over. It will be a mini family reunion,' he had insisted.

But Mrs Desai hadn't been too convinced. She had justified to her husband, 'How does Arun imagine I will understand Kathy's accent and her Americanness?'

As she stared at the postcards, Mrs Desai thought for the hundredth time how different Idaho looked from Kolkata, where she had lived her whole life. A long line of banana trees marked the perimeter of her home, their waxy and pliant leaves a rich shade of emerald and the grass beds surrounding them fat and squelchy from the continuous rain. She wondered if the Idaho grass smelled any different from the subtropical one here, or if the dew there tasted special, somehow more pure and dewy? She resolved to ask Dev this question the next time they talked over the phone. He was too polite to laugh at her, and even if he did, it would be all right.

As anyone close to Mrs Desai knew, she needed little persuasion to talk about Dev. Her friends had heard a million times about how Dev was as dear to her as her own children, Puru and Anjana, what a sharp student he'd been through his entire life, how he was constantly volunteering for social causes in spite of being a busy and successful software engineer, and how he broke Mrs Desai's heart every day now that he lived so far away in Idaho.

Mrs Desai heaved herself off the bed, wincing as her feet hit the stone-cold floor. Once again, 'guru . . . guru' rang from her lips, though this time the words sounded bitter like a curse. She owed this mantra to Arun. Older and wiser by two years, he had taught her to say 'guru, guru' when they were children. 'It will drive away the monsters,' he had said, and she had believed him. Back then, a lot of things scared her—the creaky bathroom door (guru, guru), the stray dogs that barked and snapped at her ankles every time she stepped out of home (guru, guru), and those evil-eyed crows that swooped down from trees and overhead antennas in wide arcs, bisecting the air into unequal halves (guru, guru).

But that was more than sixty years ago, when Mrs Desai was a little girl who relied on her big brother for everything. Arun was her friend, bodyguard, guide, philosopher, storyteller and co-adventurer. No matter what monsters they encountered, they had 'guru, guru' to act as their saviour. Increasingly these days, Mrs Desai wished she could turn back time and return to flying kites with Arun, fishing with him in the village pond and stealing tamarind pickle from their mother's storeroom.

Stifling a yawn, Mrs Desai walked into the study. Her husband, the maritime historian, had decorated one of the walls with an enormous sepia-tinted world map. Dr Desai had dotted it with multicoloured pins to indicate current locations of various family members and close friends, whether in India or abroad. The red, blue, green and yellow pins twinkled like a thousand plastic stars from cities as different as New Delhi, Mumbai, Bengaluru, Chittagong, Shanghai, Singapore, Bangkok, Dubai, London, Paris, Brussels, Berlin, Atlanta, New York, San Francisco and Boise. On the wall across it hung an oversized clock, antique-looking, but really, a clever modern contraption, a gift from his department at his retirement. Adjoining it were the many degrees and certificates Dr Desai had received throughout his career.

Ignoring them, Mrs Desai marched up to a third wall. Ever since Arun's death, she had been converting it into a photo gallery of sorts. Adding and updating it had become her daily ritual. While Dr Desai poured over historical scholarship at his desk, Mrs Desai would arm herself with a cup of cardamom tea, sit cross-legged on the floor and sift through memories—album after album of photographs, boxes upon boxes of memorabilia. She and Dev had collected them from Arun's apartment days after Dev had flown in to immerse his father's ashes and settle financial matters.

The photographs were mostly black-and-white— Arun as a scrawny teenager squinting against the sun, Arun balancing himself on a cycle as his younger sister chased him with her arms outstretched, Arun donned in the telltale hat and robe of a college graduate, Arun on the day of his wedding, Arun holding baby Dev, Arun with his colleagues on a trip to Paris, Arun and Dev building a sand castle on Digha beach, Arun caught laughing while standing between Dev and Kathy during their chaotic Hindu–Catholic wedding in Boise, Arun and Kathy posing like warriors, with their fishing poles held aloft like swords.

And there, right in the centre, was Mrs Desai's favourite picture of Arun. It showed him inside his study, where sunlight poured in from a side window and lent him a diffused halo of sorts. Arun's overcrowded desk staggered under the weight of notepads, books and coffee mugs packed with every kind of writing instrument in the world. The tabletop calendar said '1986', although it may or may not have been up to date. Arun wore an open-neck white shirt and sat hunched over a thick manuscript, a pencil tucked in between two fingers of his left hand and his brows knitted in concentration. Those were busy, insane days. Arun had just founded a niche publishing house, a dream he had cultivated right from his college days.

Mrs Desai hauled one of the many remaining cardboard boxes and settled down on the floor. This one was crammed with files arranged chronologically from 1990 to 2010. They looked as if they contained bills and receipts, the kind of stuff Mrs Desai didn't want to go through but had to.

She opened the first file. It wasn't full of invoices, like she had dreaded. Instead, there were letters, written by Dev to Arun. She checked the date on the first letter. July 1990. Dev's first month at boarding school.

Dear Baba,

I miss you. I miss Ma. I do not like this school. I wish Ma wasn't dead. I know you are busy, but I don't want to stay here. Please come and take me away. I miss Puru and Anjana.

Dev

Mrs Desai's fingers gently caressed each word. Her eyes prickled as she remembered those early months after the death of her sister-in-law. They had been hard for everyone, but especially for ten-year-old Dev, who had retreated into a shell. No matter how many toys, games, books or companions he was plied with, it was as if a part of him had died with his mother and couldn't be brought back. Arun had contemplated selling his publishing house to take up a less stressful job, something where he wouldn't have to travel so much or keep impossible hours. But after years of struggle, the business had finally established itself and he was quickly gaining a reputation for being a tough but fair publisher; talented new authors were seeking him out.

It was sometime in that first month that Arun had come to his sister and brother-in-law with a special request. Mrs Desai still remembered that Friday evening as if it was yesterday. Arun had walked in wearing the black blazer he lived in those days. The Desais had finished dinner; she was clearing the kitchen and her husband was telling her about his department's newest hire. Puru and Anjana— busy professionals now—were mere children then, and watching cartoon in their parents' bedroom. The evening had a stillness to it. Probably that's why every word rang out loud and clear, and gathered in the shadows like ghosts.

Arun had come to the point immediately. Would they be willing to raise Dev along with Puru and Anjana? Not forever, of course. Just for the time being. Dev needed the routine and rhythm of a steady family environment, and Arun was not in a position to provide that right now. He would write them a cheque at the start of every month that would take care of Dev's expenses. With time and patience, and given his fondness for Puru and Anjana, surely Dev would once again become a version of who he used to be when his mother was alive.

Mrs Desai buried her face in Dev's letter. As she breathed in its musty smell, she remembered how her husband had had consent written all over his face, his eyes behind his steel-framed glasses imploring her to say 'yes'. And yet, when he had glanced at her, he had known, the way you know when you live with someone for a decade and raise your children with them, that her answer would be a firm 'no'.

What had she been so afraid of that Friday evening? Why did she say no? Was she afraid of Dev? Of not meeting his standards? But he was a boy, a little boy of ten. Or did she fear she would discriminate between Dev and her own children, and ruin their affection for one another?

A thousand excuses had rolled off her mouth with ease. In a steady voice, she had told Arun that Dev was far too vulnerable. He needed the discipline of a boarding school and not an affectionate aunt trying to fit into his mother's shoes. Dev needed a fresh start, a new place, a new school and new friends.

Arun had heard her in silence. After she had finished, he had simply nodded. 'As you wish,' he had said and left. That was the first and last time he had ever broached the subject. A week later, Dev was on a train, travelling across two states to attend a private boarding school.

That was the beginning of the change. It was subtle at first, but with time it became more and more pronounced. A formality crept in, and so when Dev came over during vacations, Puru and Anjana were polite and friendly, but their earlier rambunctiousness was gone. No longer did the three of them stay up late and talk in hushed whispers while writing their own 'mystery novel', nor did they demand a continuous week of pizza–movie nights.

Dev drifted away further. He left India to study at the University of Idaho where he met Kathy. Soon after graduation, they married and moved to Boise. Every September, when Dev called to wish her happy birthday, he repeated his invitation, 'Come and see Idaho, you will love it.' But Mrs Desai's answer always remained the same, 'I can't, Dev. It's my arthritis. You know how it acts up.'

She set aside that first letter and sped through the next several files. Dev's letters made her feel like a historian, as if she had been tasked with the responsibility of reconstructing a life she knew only as an academic:

I won the chess tournament for the second year in a row, or '*Thanks for* A River Runs Through It, *although I am not sure I like it yet,'* or '*The camera will be helpful now that I am the editor of the school magazine'*. None of the letters was more than two sentences long, but Arun had saved them like they were pages of an invaluable manuscript.

The files from 1997 onwards did not contain any handwritten letters. Instead, they had printouts of emails. They marked the transformation of Dev, the college student, into Dev, the graduate student, and later, the young professional. Like his letters, his emails were short, but to Mrs Desai they narrated an entire lifetime of stories. As they had to her brother.

Not surprisingly, the last file was also the slimmest. Mrs Desai read Dev's final email, sent two days before Arun left for Idaho.

See you on the 29th. Kathy wants to take you fishing. Good luck.

Mrs Desai's eyes flew to the photograph of Arun and Kathy wielding their fishing poles while staring fiercely into Dev's camera. The words, 'guru . . . guru', slipped out again, but this time they sounded like a prayer and became a blessing. She saw Arun and Kathy's mock expressions of determination and competitiveness and thought how similar they looked dressed in caps, jeans and waterproof jackets. And just as easily, Mrs Desai imagined the three of them circling a fire and warming their hands as the flames cooked their fresh catch. She saw them with their heads thrown back in laughter, their silhouettes framed against the waters of a lake whose name she now knew by heart, and she granted herself, for the first time in twenty years, a tiny sliver of forgiveness.

SISTERS

Texas, 31 December 2018

I hear her before I see her. The gulp and heave of her breath, the drag and pull of her feet as she climbs uphill towards our cul-de-sac. I have finished watering the lawn and I am about to go back inside. The sun hasn't sunk yet, but our wasteful street lights are already aglow. It is going to be a cold night, like every other New Year's Eve here that I can remember. Any other time of the year, I wouldn't have heard her, but tonight, my neighbourhood is dead, and so every footfall is alive. The houses next to mine are empty, their inhabitants away holidaying—Puerto Rico, Casablanca, North Carolina—who knows where. I never go anywhere.

I pull back into the shadow of the holly tree. She hasn't seen me yet. But I want to see her.

She is short, not an inch taller than five feet, squat, with dark hair drooping to her shoulders. She is Hispanic; her face the exact shade of brown as many of my students. She is dressed in an ill-fitting blouse and a skirt that is too big for her. It swings on her small frame like a curtain. She and her clothes are weighed down by sweat and exhaustion. Dust blankets her shoes and her backpack looks dangerously overstuffed. Her eyes scan the neighbourhood. Her neck, too, moves rapidly, in line with her eyes. She is a bird in human clothes.

I don't have to know who she is or what she wants. From where I am crouched, my front door is ten feet away. Quietly, I take a few steps back. I extend my arm and grasp the doorknob. When I turn it, slowly, the unoiled creak cannot keep a secret. It gives me away.

She whips around so fast that I have no time to react. Her eyes lock with mine.

In less than a second, she sprints to my gate.

'Shit, shit, shit,' I mutter under my breath. No, I won't give her any money. Community college lecturers barely make a living.

An ornate silver cross, the size of a pinkie finger, hangs from her neck. 'Please, please,' she cries, grasping the wrought-iron bars of my gate. Her words, broken and uneven, like a river's path strewn with rocks, come out in a rush. 'They chase me. They chase me in town. Please. They take Jose. They burn his . . .' she points urgently at her backpack. 'Help. Please.' Her voice cracks. I can tell she hasn't had a sip of water in a while.

Even without her telling me, even without knowing her exact specifics, I know exactly what's going on. This town, where I have lived all my life, flits like a shadow on the line separating the United States from Mexico. I teach Spanish and Latin American history at Angelo Hall. My students are white and Hispanic and every possible combination in between. They have been born on this and that side of the border. For some of them, the border is merely a thing that exists, not unlike the Walmart and Target in town. For others, it's everything they don't want to talk about.

My own family has not been spared these complications. When my father died, I was six. Two years later, my mother, a tall white woman from California, fond of printed kaftans, turquoise jewellery and long necklaces, married a Latino man five years older than her. He had full lips, a head scrunched with dark curly hair and a voice made for singing. He was fluent in both Spanish and English, and it was he who insisted that I learn Spanish and I learn it well.

One afternoon, shortly after their wedding, I heard my mother crying into the phone. I guessed she was talking to Ana-Maria, her best friend in San Antonio. Mom didn't see me. She was curled up in a corner of the living-room sofa. I hid in the kitchen so I could hear what she was saying.

She kept insisting that she had married for love. Apparently, her new husband had just accused her of marrying him because she was a 'white saviour'. I remember not knowing what the term meant. I remember having to look it up.

~

The woman at my gate whimpers. When she grips the bars with both hands, I am inches from the safety of my threshold. The distance between us is so little that I can smell her. A rank combination of sweat, dirt and general unwashedness. 'Please, please?' she cries. 'Please help?'

My mouth goes dry. I think of the piles of ungraded papers waiting for me upstairs on my desk. My students had to write three-page essays on 'Feminism and Political Identity in Mexico'.

'No español,' I shake my head. 'I don't speak Spanish. I must go inside. My father . . . Papa . . . is not well.'

'Please,' she tries once more. She shakes the gate again. This time, gently. I see she has hurt her right hand. There are scratch marks all over her fingers.

I slink into my house and shut the door. I watch her through the keyhole. Her shoulders slump forward. She looks so broken, I shrink back, as if her despair can leach through my door and seep into my skin. When I look at her again, she has turned her back towards me and squeezed herself under the shadow of my neighbour's white oak tree. There is something deeply familiar about the way she has hunched her shoulders, in the complete and absolute surrender steaming off her body.

I know why it is familiar.

This is exactly how I look to others. This is how my colleagues, neighbours and students see me. And why won't they? I am a pathetic, pitiable creature. I own this two-storeyed house, and presumably the woman outside owns nothing except her backpack. Yet, she and I are not so different.

~

The first time I wished for a sister—the kind who would make funny faces with me for family photographs, braid my hair, fight with me over clothes, boys and make-up, but most importantly, protect me from the rest of the world—was the Saturday right after my eighth birthday. The streamers and balloons that Mom had put up were still in the living room, albeit they didn't look as full and fat any more. A bit of my cake was on the middle rack of the fridge. Red velvet—my favourite—with chocolate icing. Mom had got it decorated with roses and strawberries, two of my other favourite things.

We had had eggs for breakfast that morning. My yolk-stained fork and plate were in the sink. I hadn't wanted eggs. I had wanted cake. My birthday cake. Mom had said, 'No, not now.' She had said so in Spanish, so he, her new husband, wouldn't feel left out.

'You *are* a white saviour, aren't you?' I had screamed at her. 'Why do we have to speak Spanish? Why can't he learn more English?'

Mom had 'recoiled' will sound better here. Like I had slapped her. Then she had grabbed her purse—red leather with a turquoise clasp—and stormed out. 'I need some time for myself,' she had announced through gritted teeth. 'I can't keep up with who wants what from me.'

It was the first time she had left me home alone with him, my stepfather, he with the dark, curly hair, lips full of English and Spanish, and hands . . . hands like sharkskin, a creature I had just learned about in school.

~

I double- and triple-check to make sure the doors and windows are locked. I pull down the blinds. I close all the curtains. My stomach rumbles, but I don't turn on the kitchen lights. I don't need food right now. Besides, I really don't want to eat last night's quesadillas or linger a minute longer than necessary at the dining table. I consider grabbing the last pear from the fruit bowl and heading upstairs. I assure myself the woman is gone. She has left the shade of the white oak to try her luck someplace else.

~

He had entered my room minutes after Mom's car had pulled out of the driveway. Why hadn't I run after her?

Tugged at her red purse? Ripped off that stupid turquoise clasp? Why hadn't I told her over and over that I was sorry, that I would eat eggs for every meal of my life if that is what she wanted?

At first, I thought he was there to tell me to clean up the breakfast table. It was their favourite punishment for me those days. But that morning, I didn't want to do anything for anyone. All I wanted was cake. So, I screamed and screamed, but he caressed my face and quieted me down. When I told him I wanted to read one of my new books out loud, he laughed. When I fell silent, he told me to lie down on my bed.

Did I already say his hands were like sharkskin? Do you know sharkskin feels like teeth, and if you aren't careful while touching it, it can make you bleed?

I let my mind wander, and because I didn't get to read a story, I ended up making one.

I gave myself a sister. I named her Jo. Like Jo March from *Little Women*. My Jo was older than me, and in many ways, she was exactly like she was in the book. Strong and fierce, she loved to read. And she always, always stood up for her sister.

I didn't realize when I started telling him my story. I suppose I hoped he would get lost in Jo's adventures, that he would stop doing what he was doing. But that didn't happen. Because my Jo story was childish and sentimental. It was awful and silly.

I remember how his voice thickened. 'Keep talking, sweetie,' he said, 'don't stop.' His breath settled, warm and sticky.

For all those years, those mornings, afternoons and nights that bled into each other, I thought of Jo every single time. I wanted her to be real. Flesh and blood, bones and breasts, muscles, thighs, lips and soft tissue. I no longer thought of Jo as my saviour. I wanted her to come to life so I could toss her into the fire, offer her up as tribute, let her take my place for a change.

~

One night, after he left my room to return to the one he shared with Mom, I got up to use the bathroom. Mom sat on the living room floor, her head bowed, her body pushed into the front door, as if she wanted to spill out of the house. She wore a pair of oversized headphones, and though I could only see the back of her head—somehow, I knew her eyes were closed.

Was she praying? I am not sure. Could she have been plotting our escape? Unlikely. By then, she had lost her job. She had stopped driving. She had cut off Ana-Maria from her life and adopted whisky. She would spend days on end in her kaftans, rarely leaving her bed, or she would stay holed up in her bathroom. I remember thinking that the headphones were like giant hands clamped over her ears. They were there to block out noises and realities she didn't want to confront.

Years later, I tried to help Mom. I tried to pull her out of the black hole she had slid into. I threw her a rope. I hoped she would reach out and grab it, but she didn't. My mother—married young, widowed young and remarried young too. Death, too, couldn't wait for later.

She left me this house. She had bought it a few years before I was born. Nothing has ever been changed here. There are still two rooms upstairs—my mother's sewing room that's now my study, and her bedroom, sealed shut since 19 January 1995, when I found her on the floor, wrists cut open, her hands liquid, like rivers.

I glance about the living room and the kitchen. I hurry past my old bedroom that I now use for storage. I sleep in the living room. On the couch. It's okay. I can do that. There is no one to pass judgement. I haven't had a visitor in twenty-one years.

~

Once upstairs, I go about straightening my desk. Pens here. Pencils there. Organized alphabetically, the student essays sit right in the centre.

A commotion, like people hooting and scuffling, draws me to the windows. I part the curtains an inch. I can't see anything. It might be from the street next to ours. It could be the usual New Year's Eve revelry. Or it could be the men chasing her.

Did I say 'men'? Or am I projecting? Do women gather in mobs and chase?

I close the curtains, pull out the chair and sit down at my desk. I put on my headphones. Tight, oversized and noise-cancelling, they are perfect.

~

The only adult who ever suspected anything was Mom's friend, Ana-Maria. During one of her visits, when I was twelve or thirteen, I remember she and Mom argued every day.

The morning she was due to leave, Ana-Maria pulled me aside. 'Darling, tell me what's wrong. You can trust me,' she had insisted.

I had smiled. A lot. I had said, 'Nothing's wrong. I am fantastic.' I already knew what happened to girls who told stories. I didn't need things to get worse. I kept hoping Ana-Maria would leave and never come again.

But she came one last time. When Mom died. Ana-Maria wanted me to leave this house and go with her. But how could I have done that? As awful as things have been for me inside these walls, everything that's outside could be far worse.

Ana-Maria had pleaded. 'Come on, darling. Please, come with me. This house is not right for you. You need a new city. You need new friends. Maybe a boyfriend. Won't that be nice? You can stay with me for as long as you like.'

I had struggled to not laugh in her face. I didn't need a new city. I could take care of myself. And I had a friend. Well, sort of. My thesis adviser. He had begged me to let him touch my breasts, and I had. We now had a standing date every afternoon, right after he finished his last class of the day and before he left to pick up his children from school.

~

There's a picture of Mom on my desk. In it, she is nineteen, shiny like a pearl and pregnant with me. The photographer, my biological father, has caught her in the middle of a laugh. Her eyes are squeezed shut, and her head is tilted to one side. I think Dad must have said something funny.

I turn up the volume on my headphones. I stare into the photograph. Dad died in a drunk-driving accident. He wasn't the one drinking. And Mom died because she picked up drinking.

Maybe.

Or maybe, she died because she wanted to leave me with a clean slate. Her second husband was already in hospice care by then. Perhaps she thought I'd never be able to forgive her, and this was her way of saying sorry. She wanted me to feel free, with no one to care for, no baggage weighing me down, and this house, an asset that I could sell, physically move away from, and begin life somewhere anew.

I don't think she realized that not having anyone to care for can weigh you down too.

~

From the windows of my study, you can see the entire length of our street. On any other day, at this hour, there would be a long line of cars, the locking and unlocking of doors, and folks going about their lives with one eye on their phones and the other on their children.

Suppose they had all been here today? Would any of them have noticed the woman in the shadows? In border towns like ours, there are hundreds of women and men, like her. They are white and brown, wealthy and poor, young and old. They hunch their shoulders and they rely on ornate silver crosses or oversized headphones to help them negotiate one day to the next. They live quiet and invisible lives until they die of old age. Sometimes, they disappear young. Others, like my mother, slit themselves open.

I take off the headphones. I switch off the desk light. Tonight, I will let the stack of essays be. I will heat up last night's quesadillas. And I will set out an extra plate. But first, I will walk around the neighbourhood. I will coax one person out of the shadows.

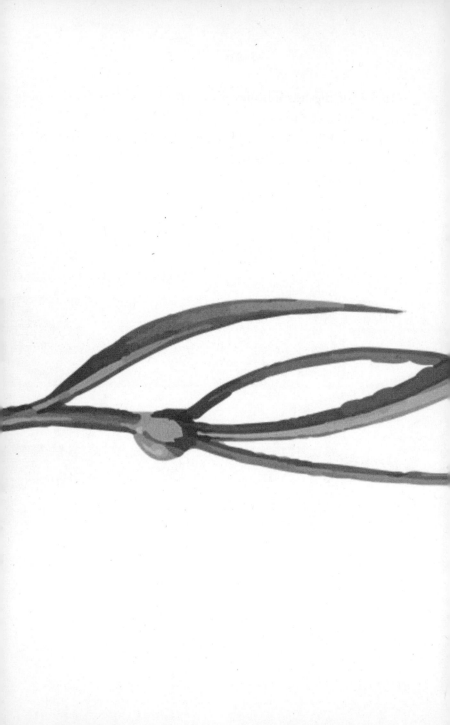

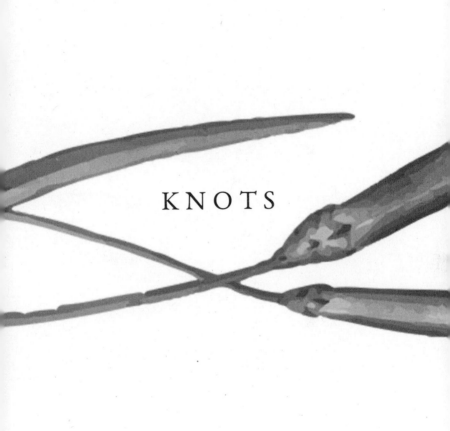

KNOTS

Calcutta, March 1948

On the morning she decides to leave her husband, Manasi props her elbows on the cracked windowsill and watches the office babus. In their crisp Western shirts and pants, about to board the buses and trams that will take them to their destinations, they are not unlike the white sahibs they served until a year ago. Except when it comes to food, perhaps. Manasi wonders if their wives have packed their lunches for them or if they will eat in canteens and coffee houses. Not sandwiches, nor puddings surely. But rice. With fried fish? Yes. And maybe a dollop of ghee on a mash of boiled eggs and potatoes, a dribble of mustard oil over roughly chopped coriander and onion with a deadly green chili tucked on the side. Or maybe rotis with dal, with a sliver of mango or tamarind pickle.

Manasi's mouth waters. She licks her lips and remembers the Sunday six weeks ago, when the landlady had climbed the two flights of stairs connecting their homes to press a brass bowl into her hands. Inside, coated in a thick yellow-brown gravy, were four small pieces of chicken. They were overcooked and stringy, and yet Manasi had attacked them ravenously. She had chewed every string of flesh, sucked out the marrow, gnawed on the bones and then crushed them down into a paste. Her husband hadn't wanted any bit of the chicken. He had merely watched her, the way one might observe a child reunited with an old, favourite toy. His eyes had held no amusement. He had, in fact, looked a little sad.

Really, why doesn't he share her enthusiasm for food, Manasi wonders, as she reaches out to rub her stomach. But like lightning, she jerks her hand away. She doesn't want to touch or acknowledge what's inside. It's not a baby. Nor a foetus. It is an embryo. That's what the doctor called it. *An embryo. About the size of a small pencil.* Odd that a conversation not even an hour old can seem so distant, as if it happened to someone else on an alien planet and she had simply been there to observe. She is amazed that she could pull herself together to ask a question. *Can we take care of it?*

She had kept her eyes trained on the doctor's polished black shoes.

Yes, he had said. He hadn't pressed her for any details. In a city still recovering from riots, pregnant women were as common as pigeons.

From a nearby home, the deep notes of a conch shell ring out. Manasi sucks in her breath. It reminds her too much of home, this announcement of daily prayer. She turns away from the window. She is glad she has made the appointment for tomorrow. The sooner, the better. She doesn't want to risk her husband finding out. He, barely twenty years old himself, will welcome the burden of fatherhood. She has already made one foolish romantic mistake in her life. She cannot afford another.

The spring sun warms her back. It puddles the floor and brightens the discoloured walls of the attic she calls home these days. Her husband won't be back for another seventy-five minutes. Should she eat? Surely he wouldn't mind. She has long since digested the two biscuits and tea he insists on calling their 'breakfast'. Or should she cook something extra, something more than their usual rice and lentils menu? Why isn't there a book of instructions on what to feed one's husband when the marriage is over? Maybe she could bargain with the fishmongers before they pack up for the day. Surely one of them will let her have an unsold fillet or two.

A woman across the street wars with the onion seller. They are both so loud that Manasi can hear every word. She doesn't have to lean out of the window to see them. They do this every day. She knows their voices. She admonishes them quietly, 'One less peel will not change the course of history.'

Her eyes sweep over their 'apartment'. The western corner of the ceiling stretches like a mossy carpet, the green skin of an ancient reptile. There is an inch-wide leak in the middle that her husband has stuffed with straw. Still, on rainy days, it drips like the tears of a new widow.

A bed, pushed against the wall, is their only furniture. It is where they sit for their meals, where her husband reclines against the wall to study for his classes, where they both prepare notes for the private tuitions they deliver, and where Manasi lies down whenever she is alone or overcome by hunger. Yes, she can stuff her face with whatever is in the kitchen, but she doesn't. Not that her husband would scold her or pick a quarrel. It's just that there is only so much to cover their meals. Anything beyond that would be wasteful.

She runs through her speech again. *I can't live like this any more. There is nothing romantic about being poor and always hungry. I'm returning to my parents' home. This marriage is over.* Cruel and careless. Yes, perhaps. And yet, what must be done must be done. A firm break with no mention of the baby. No, not a baby. An embryo, the size of a small pencil.

The cheerful red flowers of the bedspread don't fool anyone. Even now, after so many washes, the cheap dye bleeds. So in the mornings, they wake up with what looks like bruises all over their skin. The rickety frame groans under their weight although they are both slim and small-framed. They sleep tight, not just from ardour, but because if they aren't careful, one of them will roll off the bed and land on the floor.

The built-in wall closet holds their earthly possessions— Manasi's five saris pleated neatly and stacked one on top of the other, and her husband's shirts and dhotis, although his folding is far less precise than hers. She keeps their wedding garlands bundled inside a cotton handkerchief. The tuberoses dried up within two days, but she can still make out their faint outline through the thin fabric.

Tucked behind Manasi's saris is an old biscuit tin. It contains a silver bangle, a pair of pearl earrings and sixty precious rupees, of which fifty will go to the doctor tomorrow. It is the cost of his discretion. Manasi's hand strays to her stomach again. This time, she doesn't jerk it away.

She closes her eyes and the room disappears, as does the busy street outside. A pond surrounded by a grove of papaya trees appears instead. It is early morning, and the sky is a splatter of orange and purple. A girl, barely five years old, hovers at the edge of the pond. It is so deep that its waters appear black. Like the rest of the world, it too has awoken from its spent state. Bird calls erupt from around it like fireworks.

Why do we have the pond with the black water, Ma? Why do the boys have the nicer one? The girl's finger is pointed like an arrow. Her nails are yellow, battle stains of a recent mango-eating competition with her cousins. Food is everything in her world—nourishment, competition, childhood and games.

The mother clicks her teeth, a sure sign that she wants to change the topic. *Because those are the rules, Manu,* she says, as if her cryptic answer should be enough. She applies a generous helping of coconut oil on her daughter's defiant little head. *Remember this day always, Manu. The first day of school. No other girl has ever had this privilege in this family. You have to make us proud. Especially your father.*

The girl and her mother return from the pond to their home. It's a stately mansion, august and red-bricked, and over a hundred years old. The columns are covered with sweet-smelling vines. The stone floors are cool to touch. From dawn to dusk, the house reverberates with the pitter-patter of young and old feet, the jangle of keys, coins and gold bangles, but mostly the sounds of food—the sizzle of spices when they hit hot oil, the call of the fishermen who bring their fresh catch straight to the kitchen, the politics and gossip of those who cook, the hierarchy of freshly slaughtered goat as opposed to the mound of boiled potatoes for the widowed aunt.

Manasi wipes her eyes. She sees the fourteen people gathered around a large, oblong dining table. The patriarch of the family takes his seat at the head, and like always, makes the same joke.

Look at us, we are English! We have a table. We are democratic. Our men and women eat together.

Despite the repetitiveness, Manasi smiles. What a forward-thinking man. But why did he tie his dream to his daughter's destiny? Why did he insist that she too must become a doctor? His oldest son *was* already one. How many doctors does a family need?

Still, that's the home and the father Manasi wants to return to. Would he forgive her? Yes, she made a mistake. She fell in love, ran away from home and married a poet. It had seemed so magical, the way he could pluck words from the air and knot them one after the other into sentences that glowed like fireflies.

Manasi sits on their bed. She imagines the red petals of the bedspread leaking under her fingers. This is where they make love, knotted tightly into each other, their movements warm, rhythmic and hungry, just like Calcutta, new and independent, eager to announce its presence to the world. Their wedding, too, had echoed the impatience of the city. It had been the two of them and two of his friends from college—doubling as witnesses—and the sole government official, eager for his two rupees and their signatures.

Yes, *that's* what happened. They were so impatient to get married that they couldn't be bothered with invitations and planning for a formal religious ceremony. It wasn't because they couldn't afford anything besides the two garlands of marigold, a box of sweets and the shawl that one of the guests had draped over their shoulders and tied into a knot. If they had had a real wedding, that task would have gone to her sisters, and afterwards, they would have sat down for a feast.

Manasi swallows hard. Nothing in Calcutta matches the taste of fish she once ate without a second thought. Freshly caught and delivered, the rui and katla fish gleamed like silver until they arrived on the table, cooked in stone-ground mustard with coconut, ginger and green chillies.

With a bit of luck and persistence, her husband can get a decent job in Calcutta. But he doesn't want to. What he wants is time to write. He attends literature classes in the mornings, and in the afternoons and evenings, they both give private tuitions. But their meagre income barely keeps them afloat. Some nights, when she cannot bring herself to eat another bite of rice and lentils, Manasi opts to go to bed hungry.

How do others do it, she wonders? How do they stave off acute, ferocious hunger? Yes, Manasi knows gluttony is a sin. Gluttony, from the Latin *gluttire*, which means to gulp or swallow. But that's what she wants, to cast off this current life and return to the one where she can gulp it all—a soft bed, a roof that does not drip and the mouthfeel of ever-present food.

Manasi pulls the ends of her sari, and ties and unties knots into the cotton fabric. 'You look like a princess,' her husband had said the first time she had worn this sky-blue sari with its thin black border. He had bought it with his first salary. He had pulled it out from its newspaper wrap with such pride, as if he was gifting her the Koh-i-noor.

The cheap cloth had made her fingers curl with distaste. He had forgotten to remove the price tag and the sight of that paltry number had felt like a slap. Did she really need yet another reminder of their poverty? Could he not have scratched out the price?

She had swallowed the questions itching at the edge of her mouth. *Why didn't you bring us some food instead? A tiny box of sweets? Or two samosas?*

Quietly, she had stepped inside their bathroom, where, by the light of a single candle, she had pleated the sari, straightening and smoothening each fold until it was tight and crisp, the way her mother had taught her. She had brushed and braided her hair and stepped out, flushed and light-headed. No, not because of the reaction she anticipated from her husband but because she had been without food for far too many hours.

He had been standing by the window, humming an old song from their village, and staring at the men and women who would work their way into his poems. At the sound of her footsteps, he had turned to look at her. For several seconds, he had stood like that, his arms folded, his gaze flitting from one inch of her body to another. 'You are so beautiful,' he had whispered, his voice infused with desire.

That memory now makes Manasi's heart ache. She counts the sacrifices her husband has made to be with her. He has been thrown out of his father's will. His sister writes to him often, reminding him of his 'selfishness' and how he has besmirched the family's name.

But is this sacrifice enough? Is his nobility such a badge of honour that she must wear it all her life? Four months ago, she was the pampered eighteen-year-old daughter of a wealthy businessman, and today, she is the famished nineteen-year-old wife of a struggling poet.

'Sorry,' she whispers to her stomach. She imagines the horrified reactions of her family, if they ever found out what she had planned for the next day.

Another conversation dredges up in Manasi's memory. It had occurred at the dining table back home, with her father at his usual spot. Everyone else had left.

'Do you know what a conventional father would do?' his voice had carried resignation.

'Lock me up until I promise to marry a boy of his choice.'

'I have never raised a hand on you. Not once. You were going to be the first female doctor in our family. What happens to that dream now?'

'Medicine is not for me, Baba. He is.'

'You are shameless. You have a fine brain. Why are you throwing it away?'

'I love literature.'

'You love literature because that fool loves literature. Go away. You have said enough.'

Manasi buries her face in her hands. She weeps noisily. Tears and snot drip into her fingers and find their way into her sari. Whatever happened to that love for literature? Is it enough to listen to poems every night, to fall off to sleep to their cadence? In the glare of the morning, a poem does not pay rent. It does not buy fish nor rice. It does not let her pack a nice lunch for her husband or pick quarrels with onion sellers.

She rises from the bed and wipes her tears. Inside their two-shelf kitchen, she pulls out the leftover rice and adds a spoonful of lemon pickle to it. The first bite is too salty— whether from the oil or her tears, she cannot tell. She pushes the plate aside.

Outside their window, the buyers and sellers of the bustling market have fallen silent. The stores have downed their shutters for the afternoon. She scoops up two potatoes from the wicker basket. A few fries will add crunch to the rice and lentils. For a second, she pauses and relaxes her hold on the potatoes. How will her husband react if she tells him the news? He, who cannot provide the basics for their present, will get dreamy about their future. He will want to name it, this embryo they have created, no bigger than a small pencil.

A sound on the ground floor alerts Manasi to her present. She narrows her eyes as she tries to listen intently. She hears the key turning in the front door, followed by the flap-flap-flap of dusty sandals, the straps held together by sheer willpower and prayer.

She opens the door to their little flat and cranes her neck. It's him. He is at the foot of the stairs, hovering by the letterbox, checking their afternoon mail.

She studies him the way one might study a stranger. He is an ordinary man, dressed in a frayed blue shirt and a white dhoti. A wayward leaf has tangled itself in his thick wavy hair. If they had been two strangers and she had walked past him on the street, she wouldn't have turned around for a second look. Not once. He is that ordinary. Unremarkable. Just another struggling poet in the streets of Calcutta. How long will words keep him alive?

He takes the stairs but doesn't look up. Manasi tightens her grip on the potatoes. She imagines platters of biryani and deep bowls of snowy, sweet roshogolla. She inhales deeply.

Now, he looks up. There are eight steps left. He takes them two at a time, though it's only been a few hours since he last saw her. He breaks into a smile as if they are going to enjoy a massive feast and not merely rice and lentils, first for lunch and again for dinner. He doesn't know whether she has had time to fry any potatoes or bargain with the fishermen for cheap fillets.

His blue shirt smells of Calcutta's dust and smoke. He smells different at night when he begs her to listen to a revised poem or when he pulls her into their bed.

A knot forms in her stomach, but Manasi steadies herself. She leans against the door. No poem has ever nourished anyone. No smiles have ever replaced the scent of basmati served with a slow roasted rack of lamb. She deserves a lot more—a doting father, a doctor brother, a full house, conversations with her mother, meals with her extended family gathered around an enormous dining table and bed sheets that won't stain her hands every night.

Manasi opens her mouth. She says, 'I am pregnant.'

ACKNOWLEDGEMENTS

I will start by thanking Trisha Bora, who emailed one day and asked, 'What's happening with your stories?' I am grateful for your help and wish more power to you, your plants and your green thumb.

Thanks to Aparna Kumar and Manasi Subramaniam, my extraordinary editors at Penguin Random House India. You responded warmly to these misbehaving women and gave them a home, and you answered each of my 18 million questions with patience, grace and good humour.

Love and hugs to the many amazing women who have mentored me over the years: Kim Barnes, Joy Passanante, Omita Goyal, Manmeet Mann, Anshu Dogra, Veena Sachdev, Upinder Singh, Anita Krishan, Jyoti Bisht, Usha Koshy and Annie Mavely. Gratitude to the friends I hold dear, who I consult before every important decision, be it writing or otherwise, and whose support I feel whether they be near or far: Annie Lampman, Manasi Kanuga, Shardul Kerkar, Parul Pal, Suvena Bansal, Smita Naha, Rajarshi Sengupta, Jeff and Jane Jones, Brandon and Kelli Schrand, Mike Filipowski, Ron McFarland and Georgia Tiffany, Brittney and Andy Carman, Jordan Hartt, Katie Farris, Kelly Roberts, Sunaina Mathur Dalaya, Aruni Kashyap, Rohit Talwar and Subhadip Purakayastha.

To my awesome colleagues and students at the University of North Carolina Wilmington, talking books and writing with you is one of the greatest joys and privileges of my life. Thank you for energizing and inspiring me every day.

To my brother, Aritro, and my sister-in-law, Ashmita, love, best wishes and hugs, plus all the cocktails and kebabs of the world. No storytelling session is ever complete without the robust presence of my uncle and aunt, Saumyabrata and Nabanipa Sengupta. To them, and my cousin Sinjini, endless cups of tea and ice cream, but maybe not at the same time!

Thanks to my parents—Swapna and Atanu Dasgupta—for my happy childhood. It was filled with books, good food and great people. I am buoyed by your relentless faith in me and support for my work. The older I get, the more I realize what gifts I have in you.

To my long-suffering husband, Amrinder Singh Grewal, all my love and gratitude. Thank you for cooking me cauldrons of biryani, for buying me books upon books and for taking me to lighthouses and lavender farms. I love your intelligence, good heart, patience and generosity. I thank you for laughing at my jokes and for liking misbehaving women. And, fine . . . the Seattle Seahawks rule!

And finally, to nonconformist women everywhere, including both my grandmothers—Chhaya and Minati Dasgupta. This book is for you.